Gail Hamilton

A Battle of the Books

Recorded by an unknown writer for the use of authors and publishers. Edited and

published by Gail Hamilton

Gail Hamilton

A Battle of the Books
Recorded by an unknown writer for the use of authors and publishers. Edited and published by Gail Hamilton

ISBN/EAN: 9783337219581

Printed in Europe, USA, Canada, Australia, Japan

Cover: Foto ©Andreas Hilbeck / pixelio.de

More available books at **www.hansebooks.com**

A

BATTLE OF THE BOOKS,

RECORDED BY AN UNKNOWN WRITER,

FOR THE USE OF

AUTHORS AND PUBLISHERS:

TO THE FIRST FOR DOCTRINE, TO THE SECOND FOR REPROOF,
TO BOTH FOR CORRECTION AND FOR INSTRUCTION
IN RIGHTEOUSNESS.

EDITED AND PUBLISHED BY

GAIL HAMILTON.

"Why talk so dreffle big, John,
Of honor, when it meant
You didn't care a fig, John,
But jest for *ten per cent?*"
BIGLOW PAPERS.

CAMBRIDGE:
Printed at the Riverside Press,
AND FOR SALE BY
HURD AND HOUGHTON, NEW YORK.
1870.

CONTENTS.

		PAGE
I.	Editor's Introduction	1
II.	Author's Introduction	7
III.	Rise and Progress of Suspicion in the Soul	11
IV.	Declaration of War	33
V.	Skirmishing	51
VI.	A Truce	62
VII.	Renewal of Hostilities	75
VIII.	Arrangement of Preliminaries	125
IX.	Battle of Gog and Magog	155
X.	Sober Second and Third Thoughts	249

A BATTLE OF THE BOOKS.

I.

EDITOR'S INTRODUCTION.

HE papers comprising the following narrative, called "A Battle of the Books," were found in my state-room after a violent storm, during a long and dangerous sea-voyage which I was once forced to undertake. They were much stained with salt-water, but were for the most part legible. The name of the author or compiler is not given; but I judge, somewhat from the chirography, chiefly from incontestable internal evidence, that the writer is a woman. As this evidence will unfold itself to the reader in the course of the narrative, I shall not dwell upon it; nor is it, indeed, a matter of importance, except as it bears upon the question of the participation in the government by both sexes. Viewed from that point, it shows with great force the inability of women to understand affairs, and the groundlessness of the

1

present clamor for a change of status. It proves beyond question that all that women need do is to trust, and all that men care to do is to protect.

The date given is of the last century, but of its accuracy I am not assured. The manuscript is soiled, and stained, and shabby enough; but the storm which brought it to my feet would account for that. There are references, allusions, and even names which point to a time far within the memory of men still living; but this is not conclusive, since I believe, according to the best scriptural exegesis, the name of a historical person in a book, as, for instance, that of Cyrus in Isaiah, does not determine the date, so much as the nature of the writing, simply changing it from history to prophecy. No one, in reading this story, will suspect it of scriptural inspiration; but may not the writer have been in that state which is sometimes called clairvoyant, and which is perhaps but a preternaturally acute condition of the intellectual perceptions, wherein the logic of events is so plainly seen that the future is as clear and certain as the past, and that which is to happen seems as much a matter of fact as that which has happened? If the human mind can calculate an eclipse of the sun, with entire accuracy, three thousand years beforehand, why should it be thought a thing incredible that the human heart should be able to calculate some of the incidents of an eclipse of faith a hundred years in advance?

But as upon the question of authorship, so upon that of chronology, I conceive the strongest evidence to be internal. The state of society described in this narrative is surely no nearer than a hundred years. It chronicles an age of barbarism, when author and publisher were natural enemies, and relieved the monotony of their lives by petty skirmishing or pitched battles with each other. This age, happily for us, has passed away, and exists only in tradition. Whether from the universal softening of manners which accompanies the introduction of Christianity, and in which both publishers and authors may be supposed to have shared, or from that equally universal brightening and quickening of the intellect which attended the Renaissance, and which may have enabled even publishers to see how he that watereth shall be watered also himself, — certain it is that these times of turbulence are gone, and we have peace. No longer does the wily publisher lie in wait, seeking what chance he may have to devour his author. Rather he woos him to receive his dues, wins open with gentle urgency the hand no longer grasping, but modest and reluctant, and presses into it the crisp, abundant bills. No longer do authors shamelessly drink toasts to the despotic emperor to whose thousand crimes is linked the one virtue of having hanged a bookseller. On the contrary, they raise their harps

and join voices to sing their benefactor's praise.
Who has not seen in all the newspapers the affect-
ing tale of the great house of Fields, Osgood, & Co.,
— *nomen clarum et venerabile,* — on whom has fallen
the mantle of Ticknor & Fields?

"Fame spread her wings, and with her trumpet blew"

the story of their having offered payment to an
author, which he declined to receive because he had
once had money for the writing. "But," replied
the firm, " we intend to use the article for a book.
We make a profit on both.   Why should you
hesitate to take pay?"   "I am sure I ought not to
take it," said the author; "I should not if I acted
according to my ideal.   I don't believe it is honest
to take money twice for the same piece of work."
"But do," replied the publisher; "we insist upon
it as our right;" and insist he did, till the author
coyly yielded.   History is silent from this point, but
the imagination fondly stoops to trace the scene.
Undoubtedly this prince of publishers, like Mr.
Pecksniff when blessing Martin Chuzzlewit for
hating him, "waved his right hand with much
solemnity. . . . There was emotion in his manner,
but his step was firm.   Subject to human weak-
nesses, he was upheld by conscience."

Hear also what the " Atlantic Monthly " says:
" There are no business men more honorable or

more generous than the publishers of the United States, and especially honorable and considerate towards authors. The relation usually existing between author and publisher in the United States is that of a warm and lasting friendship, — such as . . . . now animates and dignifies the intercourse between the literary men of New England and Messrs. Ticknor & Fields. . . . . The relation, too, is one of a singular mutual trustfulness. The author receives his semi-annual account from the publisher with as absolute a faith in its correctness as though he had himself counted the volumes sold. . . . . We have heard of instances in which a publisher had serious cause of complaint against an author, but never have we known an author to be intentionally wronged by a publisher. . . . . How common, too, it is in the trade for a publisher to go beyond the letter of his bond, and after publishing five books without profit, to give the author of the successful sixth more than the stipulated price."

Time and scissors would fail me to cull from the journals all the ingenious and touching paragraphs which show how the eminent publishers referred to do good by stealth and blush to find it fame.

Doubtless similar illustrations might also be drawn in great numbers from other sources, were ordinary publishers in the courtly habit of keeping a his-

torian to record their royal deeds. But enough has
been said to show that the publishers of to-day have
become evangelized, and no longer seek every man
his own, but every man the things of another. I
infer, therefore, without hesitation, that the dates of
the following papers are correct, and that, notwithstanding a certain confusion in the nomenclature,
the state of things they describe, belongs exclusively
to the good old times of a hundred years ago.

Joined to the main body of the narrative were
injunctions the most imperative regarding its publication. But even had I chosen to disregard these,
there are other reasons which might have impelled
me to the same course. As one sitting by his own
fireside glows with a deeper content for the sound
of the storm without, so we, who live in this golden
age of love, may all the more rejoice, seeing how
they let their angry passions rise in the brave days
of old.

I would say, then, borrowing the language of an
old Sunday-school hymn : —

> " Authors, attend, while I relate
>   A new and simple story;
>   'Twill teach your hearts with thankfulness
>   To praise the Lord of glory "

that the lines have fallen to you in pleasant places,
and that you receive your goodly heritage without
having to fight for it.

II.

WHEN. in the course of human events, it becomes necessary for an author to dissolve the bands which have connected him with his publishers, a decent respect for the opinions of mankind requires that he should declare the causes which impel him to the separation.

The war between authors and publishers has been a conflict of ages. On the one side, the publisher has been looked upon as a species of Wantley dragon, whose daily food was the brain and blood of hapless writers.

> "Devouréd he poor authors all,
>   That could not with him grapple;
> But at one sup he ate them up,
>   As one would eat an apple."

On the other side, the author has been considered, like Shelley, "an eternal child" in all that relates to practical business matters, and a terrible child at that, — incapable of comprehending details, and unreasonably dissatisfied with results. A definite

illustration will sometimes throw more light on a
general principle than reams of abstract discussion.
But in matters of this sort, definite illustrations are
very hard to come at.   In any case of trouble between author and publisher, it is for the interest of
the latter that it be kept as quiet as possible.   Even
if he be unquestionably right, and the difficulty be
owing solely to the author's inexperience and im-
practicability, the ill odor of having had a quarrel
will hardly be neutralized by any knowledge of its
causelessness.   The sympathy of the public is more
likely to be with the author than with the publisher.

The author also is held to silence by various considerations.   The difficulty of getting at the real
state of the case, and the misgiving which results
from it; the always unpleasant nature of the controversy; the obtrusion of one's private affairs, as if it
were a theme of general interest; the uncertainty
of any good to be obtained; the fatigue and disgust
of the quarrel itself, — a thousand circumstances
combine to make it appear altogether easier and
better to let the matter go than to take the trouble
of any adequate presentation or explanation of it.
But as he is never quite satisfied, he can never
quite let it go; and though there come not a real
thunder-storm crashing among the hills, but clear-
ing the skies, there are low mutterings and occasional flashes, which betoken a signal discontent of
the elements.

Thus exists the chronic feud between authors and publishers; partly traditional, partly experimental; a matter often for outward jest, but quite as often of deep and serious import. It is a sort of bushwhacking, in which every man whacks on his own account, and frequently does not know that there is any other bushwhacker than himself. So the warfare goes on, but to no end. Nobody learns wisdom from another man's experience, because the other man keeps his experience to himself.

I propose to supply what the theologians call a "felt want," and to become the historian of a contest all of which I saw, and part of which I was. From the confusions of long misunderstanding I would fain evolve an intelligent and lasting peace. "When," in the language of Dr. Johnson, "I am animated by this wish, I look with pleasure on my book, however defective, and deliver it to the world with the spirit of a man that has endeavored well." If it be instigated by any other motive than pure benevolence, the fact will doubtless appear in its progress. Should my little cask of oil be poured out in vain upon the stormy waters, — should I, instead of soothing their rage, be whelmed beneath it, — there remains the consoling assurance that no one else is involved in my fate.

It would be hypocritical to apologize for the intrusion of private affairs upon public notice, when it is notorious that there is nothing the public so dearly loves, nothing upon which it so eagerly fastens, nothing which it so greedily devours, as private affairs. Indeed, the privacy of affairs seems to be sometimes the only element of interest they possess, and the delight which the public finds in them is proportioned to the amount of good manners it was necessary to sacrifice in order to get at them.[1]

I give fair warning that this narration is not intended to be of interest or value to any but authors and publishers. A log-book is not generally considered very entertaining reading, yet it may be scanned with great eagerness by those who are following the track it chronicles. This is simply the log-book of a desperate voyage, a careful knowledge of which may prevent many a young mariner from being drawn into it himself.

---

[1] The most casual observer will readily see that this strain of remark can refer only to a far distant past. If our age is remarkable for any one thing, it is for a delicate reticence regarding what is not lawfully, and by divine right, its own. — *Note by Editor.*

III.

RISE AND PROGRESS OF SUSPICION IN THE SOUL.

Y relations with the house of Brummell and Hunt began somewhere about the year 1760. Until 1768 these relations had always been agreeable. I seemed to be living in an orchard of pomegranates, with pleasant fruits. I thought, as Mr. Tennyson remarked to the lily, "there is but one" publishing house, and that is the house of Messrs. Brummell & Hunt. All others were to me outside barbarians, mercenary hirelings, mere hewers of wood and drawers of water. Messrs. Brummell & Hunt published on high moral grounds, from love of literature and general benevolence. Gingerbread followed their virtue, indeed, but had no part nor lot in it. My dealings were with Mr. Hunt, and the business aspect of our connection came to be nearly lost sight of behind the veil of friendship. Money arrangements I left entirely to him. I never stipulated for anything, either on books or magazine articles. I considered that he best knew the money value of these things, and that, as we are constantly told, the interest of author and that of publisher are one. He accordingly paid me whatever he chose, and I was entirely satisfied.

One day in December, 1767, happening to want more money than was due me,[1] I recollected having seen, a few weeks before, an article in the " Segregationalissuemost,"[2] on the " Pay of Authors," which said : —

" In regard to books, the common percentage paid by publishers to average writers is *ten per cent. upon the retail price of the book;* the copies given to the press for notice not being included in the estimate. Thus, for an edition of a volume whose retail price is $1.00, the account would be made up thus : Suppose 1,000 copies to be printed, of which 90 are distributed to the press, and otherwise given away for notice, and the balance sold, the publishers would owe the author (1,000 — 90 = 910 copies, at 10c. each) $91.00. And so proportionately for larger works at costlier prices."

Without the least presentiment of anything uncanny, I made the following reference to it in a letter to Mr. Hunt. This extract unfolds the beginning of sorrows.

---

[1] A circumstance which at once relegates this story to the last century. — *Note by Editor.*

[2] Proof that this paper belongs to an age when people had time to pronounce long words. — *Ed.*

" Now see, in the ' Segregationalissuemost,' this very morning, I saw an article about the pay of authors, in which it said that the ordinary price for average authors was ten per cent. on the retail price of the book ; but according to my account I don't have ten per cent. I only have somewhere about seven or eight per cent. Looking in my papers, I find that all the contracts I have are only for fifteen cents on the two-dollar volumes, which certainly is not ten per cent., except the first contract for ' City Lights,' which says ten per cent., but the bills or accounts, or whatever it is, are made out for that, — not at ten per cent., but, just as the other, fifteen cents on the volume. At least, this is the way I make it out ; but I am not good at figures, and may have made some mistake. However, here are the papers, and you can see for yourself, or I will show them to Judge Dane when I go to Athens. I don't like to talk about it here at home any way. But perhaps you will know all about it from what I have said, and perhaps it is all right. But certainly I am an ' average writer,' and you are an ' ordinary publisher,' not to say extraordinary ! And I want all the money I can possibly·get and more too ! Especially —— dollars by and by.

" It just occurs to me that you may possibly think that I think that *you* have been falling into temptation ! My dear friend and fellow-sinner, if you should stand up with both hands on your heart, and swear that you had cheated me, I should not believe you. I should say, 'Poor fellow, work and worry have done their work. His brilliant intellect —— I saw a lovely private asylum in Corinth. I would go there and spend the summer!'

" Yours, sane or insane,

" M. N."

I waited nearly two weeks, and then, receiving no reply to this letter, I wrote to my friend, Mr. Jackson, a book-publisher of Corinth, asking him several questions, but avoiding as far as possible any personality, or giving rise to any suspicion. I hoped he would think I was merely collecting information. On the 16th of January, nearly three weeks after my letter was sent, came a reply from Mr. Hunt, in which the only reference to my inquiry was : —

" I have not answered your last letter, touching the terms expressed in the contracts ; for you and I went over that matter once, and it was with your entire concurrence with our views, based upon the present state of trade and manufacture, that the amount was decided on. When you come to town, we will go all over it again, and it will be again settled to your entire satisfaction."

This reply did not meet my question. I was aware that I had concurred in their views, as my

name on the contract showed it. But I was not
aware of ever having gone over the matter; and
I did not care for a second settlement while I
was as yet unassured of a first. I wrote again,
replying also to an invitation by telegram received the same day from a member of Mr. Hunt's
family.

"My dear Mr. Hunt:

"That is great of you to come down here with
a gay letter, and utterly blink out of sight the fact
of your having made me wretched for three weeks
by not writing. *Of course* I concurred in your
views. If you had said to me, ' Owing to the state
of trade and manufactures, all the trees are now
going to be bread and cheese, and all the rivers
ink,' I should have said, ' Yes, that is a very wise
measure.' I don't remember ever talking the thing
over with you, but I dare say I did, — or, rather,
you talked, and I nodded, as usual! And of course
I agreed; for here are the contracts that say so,
and if I don't know what is in those contracts and
accounts, it is not for want of patient industry. If
I had as many dollars as I have pored over those
miserable papers the last two weeks, I would build
a meeting-house. Don't you see the trouble lies
back of the contract? Why did you *wish* me to be
having seven or eight per cent. when other people

are getting ten ?   If it was because I was not worth
more, you need not be afraid to say so.   I can bear
a great deal of rugged truth.   But why am I not
worth more, when there is not a paper of any standing in the country, to put it rather strongly, that
has not applied to me to become a contributor,
offering me my own terms ?   Does not that show
that I have at least a commercial value ?   Writing
books seems a more dignified thing than writing
newspapers, but in point of money there is no comparison to be made.[1]   I could have got five times
as much by putting ' Cotton-picking ' in the form
of letters as I have from the book.

 " When day after day went by, and you did not
write, I came to the conclusion that your High
Mightiness was standing on your dignity, and then
I was indignant too.   I can always be a great deal
more angry with any one than any one is with me,
and I always *will* be.   And I said last week, ' If he
does not write me by Saturday, I will do something.'
And what I did was — write to Mr. Jackson.
Now you will perhaps be vexed at this, but you
have no right to be.   Do you think I am going to
die, and give no sign ?   Mr. Jackson is an older
friend than you, — I said an older soldier, not a
better ! — and then you did not write.   I did not

---

[1] This was in reference to Mr. Hunt's repeated injunctions that I should
write only books.

mention your name, nor say anything about myself or my affairs, only asked some general questions. I tell you this because your letter was good-natured. If it had been cross, I would not tell you anything; and if you will be as perplexed and uneasy for three weeks as I was, and not do anything worse than that, I will award you a gold medal. Mr. Hunt, you ought never under any circumstances to be angry with me. In your large circle of friends you may have scores who will bring you more personal revenue; but for the quality of loyalty 'pure and simple,' you will not find many who will go beyond me. I may be infelicitous and inexplicable in demonstration, but I was never anything but thoroughly true in mood.

"The telegram came this morning in due season. A thousand thanks for her kind remembrance, but of course I was not going to Athens with your letter staring me in the face. Talking it over is the very thing I don't want to do. There is nothing to be talked over. There are the papers. I admit them all. But when ——— takes you to task for some misdemeanor, — and if ever you go to the good place, it will be because that woman has pulled you through, — you don't say, 'What are you talking about? When I offered myself to you, did you not say you would have me for better, for worse; and are you not perfectly satisfied?' She

2

was satisfied then according to her lights, but doubtless she has thought twenty times since she might
have done better.   Any way, you don't 'dast' ask
her and see.   Now my case is not parallel.   'England, with all thy faults, I love thee still.'   I cannot
conceive of anybody being a better publisher than
you, because you don't seem like a business man,
but a friend.   But here is the fact that I want [so
much] and I have only [so much] to get it with, and
sales falling off, and I getting on what is sold less
than an unknown author gets on his first book.
Can you tell in a month whether the new book is
going to sell or not?   I have another children's
book nearly ready, but I suppose decency demands
an appreciable interval between two issues.   Do
you suppose the unpopularity of my doctrines has
anything to do with it?   If it has, I will thunder
them out harder still.   If I must go down, I will go
down, like the *Cumberland*, with a broadside volley.

"Of the books I want I don't know how many,
— a dozen or two.   If people won't buy them, I will
give them away, for read them they shall. . . . .

"I will now close this short note with the reflection which I have often made, — Be good, and you
will be happy.   And never bring up against me a
concurrence of views at any past time as a fortifica-
tion against *dis*currence in the present.   And if that
is, like Saint Paul, hard to be understood, — good

enough for you for not writing me sooner, and throwing me into such a perturbation. Remember always the difference between the assent of indifference and the assent of conviction. Whatever I agreed to in times past was because I had no interest whatever in the subject, and supposed it was all according to the laws of the Medes and Persians. Now that ruin gapes before me, and I am, after all, only the law unto myself, it makes no atom of difference to me that I have not been fighting you the last century — steady.

" While I am in a spasm of comparative serenity, I will declare and affirm that you are and always have been one of the kindest, brightest, and most agreeable of men ; that you never said to me a word of compliment, or silliness, or impatience, or anything that wounded me, — and Heaven knows you have said bad things enough, — and this you may cut out, and show to men and angels when we come to blows. The worst thing I ever knew you to do was not answering my last letter, and then *aggravating* me by coming down as breezy and cheery as if nothing had happened. Give my love to ———. She deserves a better fate, but I don't know that I can do aught to forward it."

Mr. Hunt's reply to this letter was through another person ; in which reply the only response to my letter was : —

" I sent off my telegram with perfect unconsciousness of your state of mind, or of the fact that there
was any business unsettled which might be talked
about.   Your note last night was a surprise, and
your non-appearance a disappointment. . . . .

" Do you forget that a certain friend of ours cannot write a word with his own hand ?   Do you
wonder, matters having been many times explained,
that he thought they must sooner or later explain
themselves through your memory ?

"*We* forget how in a retired life things work in
the mind, and you must therefore forgive the apparent neglect of one who is overwhelmed by letters
and people from day's beginning to day's end."

This reply was not soothing.   The suggestion
that one is morbidly suffering mole-hills to rise into
mountains is not flattering to his intellectual calibre.
Nor is it agreeable to be assigned the part of one
who had been so given to dissatisfaction that it was
not worth while to try to quiet him again.   One
thing I did learn from it, — that Mr. Hunt did not
design to answer my question.

I none the less desired an answer.   I thought if
I could not secure it, perhaps some one else could.
Mr. Dane was an old friend of Mr. Hunt's, and a
friend of mine.   His office was but a short distance
from Mr. Hunt's.   He had chanced to write me
some excellent advice about saving money just be-

fore, — without, however, any knowledge of this
affair. I wanted somebody's opinion, and I could
not talk about the matter. I therefore wrote to
Mr. Dane a letter of self-justification, not to say
glorification, — saying : —

"You think, perhaps, because I have once or
twice lost a few things, therefore I take no heed of
anything. On the contrary, there is probably no
one in the land who, on the whole, is more careful,
systematic, and provident than I! Truth! . . . .
There is no such thing as independence, or dignity,
scarcely honesty, without money. Perhaps that is
putting it a little too strong, but at any rate *impecu-
niosity* is a constant temptation.

"I should have . . . . more if I had had ten
per cent. on the books, as the ' Segregationalissuemost ' said the other day was the custom for new
authors. I don't. I have only fifteen cents on a
two-dollar book, and ten cents on a dollar-and-a-half
book, which is not nearly ten per cent. ; and if you
can tell me any reason why I should not have as
much as an unfledged author, I wish you would put
up your patents and do it. . . . . I want money
just now extremely. If I had a few thousand dollars, I could benefit some very excellent persons
certainly, and in all probability should lose nothing
myself, but in the course of a few years, by the
time I should want my money at least, have it all

back. I *can* take up bonds to be sure, and I
rather think I shall : but as a general thing, one
never wants to meddle with money that is settled.
Don't you think I talk sensibly ? Don't you take
back your insinuations about my loose habits of expenditure ?   Unthrift, reckless expenditure, improv-
idence, indicate an organic defect of character. But
I will not sacrifice the present to the future. 'The
present, the present, is all thou hast for thy sure possessing.' Whenever I see an imminent need, I will
not pass it by on the score of laying up for a rainy
day. For, don't you see, when the rainy day comes,
I may not be here to be rained on, while to my
friend the rainy day is already come. I will enjoy
money as I go along, — not in so reckless a way
as to involve the necessity of one day imposing
a burden upon others. And of all enjoyment, I
know of none so delightful and inexhaustible, and I
may say so marvelous, as to see the amount of relief, the quantity of sunshine and help, put into
another's life by the judicious bestowal of even a
very little money.[1]

---

[1] The editor cannot allow this sentiment to go out into the world unchallenged. To him few things are more marvelous than the amount
of provender which the ill-favored and lean-fleshed kine will consume
without giving any sign of feeding. Poverty, or incapacity, which in
this country is the almost inseparable companion of permanent poverty — poverty is a sort of Chatmoss into which cart-loads of gravel
may be upset without giving any solid foundation to build on. Hor-

" Did you ever see such a letter as this ? It is full of me, me, me, *and* me's money ; but you began it. Your letter came down upon me just when I have been full of perplexity for more than a month, and you see I have not strength enough to keep myself to myself. You will of course consider this all confidential. You better make sure of it by destroying the letter as soon as you have read it. Yes, by all means. Seems as if this letter was sort of virtuous. But you know I am not virtuous at all. And don't misconstrue me about the books. Mr. Hunt has always been everything that was generous and friendly, and I do not permit myself to admit for a moment, even to myself, that everything is not just as it should be. But that paragraph in the ' S.' induced me to examine my own papers, — joined with my great longing for money just now, — and I did not and do not understand it. Happily, it is not necessary I should. Perhaps that refers chiefly to the great Corinthian publishing houses.

MR. DANE TO M. N.

" Ten per cent. was a fair amount — I mean ten per cent. on the retail price — for B. & H. to pay you. When they put their dollar books up to two

ace Greeley was as true as the multiplication-table when he said that people generally earn money as fast as they have the ability to expend it judiciously. — *Ed.*

dollars, whether they should pay you the same percentage, should depend on their profits, and should
be a matter of honor with them.   Probably at first
they did not double their profits with their price,
but now I have no doubt they do, and more too.
Still you are very much in their hands, and it is
very disagreeable for you to help yourself.   If the
sale fell off with increase of price, although the
profit per volume was at the same percentage, they
would make less money by doing less business.

"Did you make any contract with them ever, and
what was it?

" I don't believe anybody ever gets less than ten
per cent. on *the price ;* but it may be on the whole-
sale price, which is forty per cent. off the retail —
i. e. a book that retails at $1.40 is wholesaled at
$1.00.   Pardon me, but I never imagine that a
woman comprehends what per cent. means!   Yes,
your principles are good, but your practice is probably very deficient."

M. N. TO MR. DANE.

" I am going to finish up about *my* business now,
and then I shall not ever mention the subject again.
But I did want to talk with somebody about it, having so little reliance on my own judgment.   And
your letter came just then, and so I wrote.   I have
never mentioned it to another soul.   Confucius is a

great deal better friend to me than you ever were or ever will be, but somehow I could not speak to him about it. I don't want to *speak* to any one. Besides I was afraid he would take up against Mr. Hunt.

"I have looked into my papers, but I cannot make much out of them. . . . I never thought the first thing about it till I saw in the ' S.' what I told you before — and I hardly thought of it then; but several weeks after, when I wanted money, and my account for this year was less than I expected, I hunted up the old ' S.' to see if I had read it right, and then I wrote to Mr. Hunt without thought of there being anything wrong, but asking him how it was. I supposed there was some *modus operandi,* . . . . and wanted to know what. It was nearly three weeks before he wrote again, and then came a pleasant letter; but all he said about mine was — [then follows an account of the correspondence.]

" Now I must confess I feel next door to being insulted. I hate to use the word, but there it is. ———— is as innocent and as good as an angel, and does not in the least know what she is writing about. But all that Mr. Hunt ever said to me on the subject, or I to him, did not occupy five minutes, and he never spoke but once. That was years ago. It must have been before the second contract was made. He said that owing to the fluctuations of the market, the uncertainties arising from the war, or something of that sort, they were going to give their authors a fixed sum — fifteen cents per volume — instead of a percentage. It was at a time when prices (of books) were changing from one dollar and a quarter to two dollars, but I don't know exactly when. I assented of course ; I neither knew nor cared anything about it. I had no interest in it. And that is all that has ever passed between us. Even now I have not the least fault to find if I am on the same footing as others. But why does he not say so? Do you think I am entirely unreasonable in being dissatisfied ? I wish you would tell me if you think so, for it is like death almost to think it possible that Mr. Hunt should be in the wrong. I have had the most implicit confidence in him. I like him so much that I hate to hear a word said against the 'Adriatic,' or anything that he is concerned in. I would have been delighted to write for him for nothing if he had needed the money, and asked me. . . . . Mr. Hunt's last letter to me by —— was January 18. I did not reply to it, and so the matter stands. I shall never say or do anything more about it. You cannot conceive how distasteful it is to me. Nothing in all my life — literary — ever touched me so nearly. If I had lost every speck of money that I had — twice over — it would not have so disheartened me. Confidence must be entire, or it is

nothing. Do not you ever speak to any one of this.
. . . . I shall never mention it. A dead friendship
is as sacred as a dead friend.

[But if your dead friend will not rest quietly in
his grave, but persists in stalking up and down the
earth, scaring the timid, oppressing the weak, and
boasting all the time his own beneficence, you may
presently learn with Browning, that even

" Serene deadness
Tries a man's temper."]

" Now I hope I have not overwearied you with
my tiresome letter. You need not be afraid of a
repetition of it. In fact, there is nothing more to
say, — which you will perhaps think the strongest
security of all. I hope that you are good, — at least
that you are content with nothing less than good, —
which is the highest that any of us can go, I fancy.
I think you had better burn this letter too. It will
be safest."

MR. DANE TO M. N., FEBRUARY 4.

" Let us try your case by admitted principles.
Inasmuch as you put yourself into Mr. Hunt's hands
to do what was right, he was bound to pay you as
much as others receive upon whose winnings the
same profits are made. This is Law, Gospel, & Co.
If he did more, it would be generosity; if less,
meanness or worse.

" He agreed for ten per cent. on the ' City Lights,'
and pays you fifteen cents per copy, which is exactly right if it retailed at one dollar fifty cents ; and
he pays you the same on the rest, I understand
you.

" Whether he was reasonable in asking you to
assent to the fifteen cents per copy depends on his
sales. If they were very small, he would make
less than if large. I suppose you own the copyright,
but he owns the stereotype plates, which cost the
same whether many or few copies are printed. If
when paper, and so forth, increased in value, he increased the price *pro rata*, and the sales continued
the same, he made a larger profit, and should pay
you more ; that is, your percentage should continue
as large. Now, if he sends you any proper accounts
of sales, they will tell the story as to the number of
copies sold, but not whether they cost fifty or a
hundred per cent. more than formerly. Jackson or
any book-publisher would know as to that.

" It would seem that you have received the minimum price, according to Jackson and the Segregationalissuemost, and my own notions. Your books
are well printed on tinted paper, and your *notions*
may have abridged the profits. I mean you may
have required expensive editions, more so than was
profitable ; but I think not. Will you just show
me your contracts and accounts of sales. I

am bound professionally to secresy, and my habits are fixed, so that I tell nobody other people's affairs.

" It is due to Mr. Hunt that you investigate the matter to some conclusion. . . . . Mr. Hunt mistook your position. Your ready assent to his proposition and your confidence in him, which rendered any sharp bargaining unnecessary on your part, was interpreted as inability to comprehend matters of business ; and so they said you understood it once, and will again when you are where you can be talked to. You gave no heed to what was said, and it is a waste of ink to write it all out !

" But you and I know better. Your mind is logical, and your simplicity as to business a sham."

M. N. TO MR. DANE.

" Thank you for your letter. . . . .

" Second, I don't know whether the sales were large or small. Enormous I should say, considering the quality of what was sold ; but I don't know what would be considered large as compared with other books. I remember that the ' New Zealander,' a good while ago, said that for any book not a novel five thousand was a success ; and I think all mine, or nearly all, have come up to that, and some must have gone beyond it.

" Third, I do not know who owns the copyright or the stereotype plates. I never heard anything about either.

" Fourth, I am perfectly willing to push the matter to any agreeable conclusion ; but suppose I inquire around among the publishers, and find that I have been underpaid, what do I gain ? No money, for that is all past and gone. Will it give me back Mr. Hunt? Does that strike you as sentimental ? It does me. Nevertheless, that is what it means.

" Next, it is very cool in you, if the mercury *is* below zero, — when you have always been telling that a woman has no logic, and that *I* have no logic, and other similar endearments, — to turn around now and quietly speak of my logical mind as if you had been preaching it up all your life. *I* knew it, but it is a good deal to have you even indirectly confess it. As for business, if I chose to turn my attention to it, I have no doubt I could master all its details, just as I could in cooking. But if you have a cook or a publisher for the express purpose of doing the business for you, what is the use of perplexing yourself about it ?

" I am purposing to go to Athens next Saturday. I will gather up my papers and take them to you, if you will burden yourself with them, but it is a thankless task. . . . . But I really do not want to talk about it.

" I had yesterday a hearty sort of letter from Mr. Hunt. He says that an unusual interest ever since the day of publication of ' The Rights of Men ' was

evident on all hands ; that elaborate newspaper
notices have followed the book in profuse showers ;
and though business is singularly slow this season,
he thinks it will have a good sale. He also says,
‘ When you come again, remember if there are any
business matters to be set right, we are to do it then,’
and ‘ When the juvenile book is ready, pray send it,
for it takes some time to have illustrations made,
and we are even now preparing for autumn.’

" Now that does not read like a man who is conscious of anything blameworthy. It would be impossible he should go on talking as pleasantly, and
cheerily, and carelessly as if nothing had happened,
if anything *had* happened. Doesn't it look so to
you ? And why should it be ? Brummell and
Hunt are famous for their generosity and liberality,
and what motive could they have in changing their
course for me ? It seems to me like an ugly dream.
I wish I never had thought of it at all. They could
not have been any worse off, and I might have been
better."

MR. DANE TO M. N.

" You throw yourself unreservedly into the arms
of your publishers. Few of us can safely be trusted
so far. Mr. Hunt has apparently given you the minimum share, but I do not know even that, and you
don't without inquiry. . . . . What I should do is

this, — satisfy myself that he is probably keeping too large a share, then say to him frankly, in what form you please, that it seems so, and ask him to explain. As a business matter, it is proper. As between friends, it is due to friendship. What right have you to listen to the suggestions of the adversary, and give your friend no hearing? That you don't know much of your affairs is evident, because you don't know who owns the copyright or the stereotype plates. I do happen to know, for I asked Hunt once if you retained the copyrights, and he said you did. The accounts which he should render you will show exactly the sales. Of course Mr. H. will answer verbally your letter when you meet. Why not tell him frankly just as you tell me? Don't hesitate to let me do whatever you wish done, only I don't want to be officious."

IV.

DECLARATION OF WAR.

R. Dane, at my desire, and without mentioning any names, went to several publishers in Athens, and was told by all whom he saw that ten per cent. on the retail price was the author's customary share of the profits. He was referred to Mr. Campton, of the firm of Murray & Elder, as being the person who knew more about these things than any man in Athens. Mr. C. said the same thing. I immediately wrote to Mr. Hunt, February 11 : —

"In reply to the suggestion in your last letter, that I should send my juvenile book, I am forced to say what I never thought to say, that I cannot see how it will be for my interest that you should publish any more of my books. Unhappily, it is not necessary that I should give any explanation, since the reason, if it do not exist to your own knowledge and by your own arrangement, does not exist at all."

M. N. TO MR. DANE.

" This, you see, is a little different from what I spoke of, but what is the use of keeping up appearances? If he has done what he seems to have done, there is no possible way of getting over it, and I may as well meet it face to face at once. If he takes no notice of this note, or if he asks an explanation, I shall refer him to you, and you may do whatever you think best. If he thinks this an unfriendly course, I think it is for him to show that any other was possible. Certainly, I tried hard enough to keep the matter between ourselves alone. Sometimes I feel indignant, but somehow the uppermost feeling is a sense of loss. There weighs upon me a burden, as if some great calamity had befallen. Unless he may yet show something that has hitherto not appeared, giving a new light."

M. N. TO MR. DANE, FEBRUARY 15.

" Mr. Hunt shows an indifference quite in harmony with the theory that his friendship for me is founded on his business relations. In fact, it seems that business relations and friendly relations are alike unimportant to him, for he has taken no notice whatever of my letter. Of course, I shall not be careful to preserve what he values so lightly; yet I would rather err on the side of caution than of recklessness. It is possible my letter may have been missent, or that he is out of town. Of course, when our breach becomes public, it can never be healed; and I therefore do not wish it to pass beyond us till there is no possibility of doubt. I therefore will write another note, and inclose it in this letter. If you see no objection, I should like to have you mail it to him in Athens. Then I will wait one week more. The week after, that is, the week commencing February 23, I shall wish you to call upon Mr. Hunt and get all the money, etc., of mine which he holds."

MR. DANE TO M. N.

" I am grieved and sorry with you at this thing. I thought Mr. Hunt would hasten, at the suggestion of any real dissatisfaction, to satisfy you. . . . . Yours, inclosing a note to him, just came. I know that suspense to you is very trying, and I want you to do all that is possible to keep the trouble where it is ; and I would therefore have you send him the note which you inclose, before you suggest me or any one else as a disjunctive conjunction. . . . ."

The note to Mr. Hunt simply said that I had received no answer to my last note ; that, indeed, no answer was necessary, but I should be glad to know he had received it ; and that, as it was hardly probable two successive letters should go wrong, if

I did not hear from him, I should assume that he had received both notes.

" No letter has come. . . . . There is no use in waiting. I do not understand Mr. Hunt's course, nor do I care to understand it.

" The more I think of it, the more I am inclined *not* to have you do anything about the past. Let the dead bury their dead. It will be only a disagreeable personal affair, whose sole satisfaction will be the money. It will in effect be arguing and claiming a greater value than he has set upon me. For my part, I would a great deal rather let it all go. You just call and get the money that the account says is due. Make as much of a settlement as can be settled; and if he chooses to let everything remain as it is, I choose it also. If he can afford to dispense with an explanation, so can I."

I had given to Mr. Dane an order upon Mr. Hunt for what money of mine he had in his possession.

Mr. Dane called for the money on the 24th of February, and on the same day, — but whether before or after Mr. Dane's call, I can only infer, — Mr. Hunt wrote to me : —

" Dear M. N.: —

" On my return home on Saturday, I found your note without date, informing me that you had received no reply to your ' note of last Tuesday.' I have not replied to your note of February 11th, because I could not understand the purport of it, and hoped you might be in town soon to explain it.

" In the last letter I received from you, some days before the note referred to above, written in the old friendly spirit and faith, you tell me you have a juvenile book nearly ready, and ask if it shall be sent for publication. I reply, please send it at once ; and then comes your note of the 11th inst., with this passage in it : ' I cannot see how it will be for my interest that you should publish any more of my books. Unhappily, it is not necessary that I should give any explanation, since the reason, if it do not exist to your own knowledge, and by your own arrangement, does not exist at all.' Now there must have been something in my note to you (to which this note of February 11th is a reply) which has offended you ; else why this sudden change from the sentiments in your long and friendly letter to those of the unhappy note of February 11th ? Now, pray let us understand each other ; and in all kindness, I ask you to tell me the ground of your sudden dissatisfaction.

" Very sincerely yours,

" R. S. Hunt."

Mr. Hunt's ignorance in face of my letters, his absolute inability to conjecture in what direction the trouble lay, his misgiving that some unremembered sentence in his letter had offended me, seemed to me not a little remarkable. I wrote again.

M. N. TO MR. HUNT.

" My dear Mr. Hunt : —

" It is an unpleasant story to tell, but since you desire it I will repeat it.

" You recollect the letter I wrote you some time last December, and the question I asked you in it. The ' long and friendly letter,' of which you speak, told you of my waiting, and of my writing to Mr. Jackson. Mr. Jackson's letter confirmed the statement of the Segregationalissuemost. He said, ' There is a custom of the trade which obtains for the first venture of an author unknown to fame, to receive ten per cent. on the retail price of the books after the first thousand copies are sold. . . . . As to the price per volume of M. N.'s works, I should think twenty to twenty-five cents per volume would be the fair copyright. Sometimes a moderate copyright makes larger sales by enabling the publishers to give larger discounts to the trade,' etc., etc. I still supposed there was some good reason for my receiving a lower rate than any he mentioned, and in my long letter I tried to make clear to you the point which I wished settled. In your reply, you said, by E——, ' Do you wonder, matters having been many times explained, that he thought they must sooner or later explain themselves through your memory ? *We* forget how, in a retired life, things work in the mind,' etc., etc. My memory is not wont to play me false ; and so far from matters having been many times explained, they have not been explained at all. I have never so much as sought any explanation till now. Never but once has the subject been referred to between us. That was years ago, soon after the publication of ' City Lights,' and while prices were as yet unfixed. You then said, of your own accord, that owing to fluctuation of prices and general uncertainties, you were making arrangements with your authors to pay them fifteen cents a volume instead of a percentage. To this I readily assented. All that you said did not take five minutes, and all that I said did not amount to five words. I had a great deal more faith in your honorable intentions toward me than I had in my literary power to serve you. I had far more anxiety lest I should make you lose money, than I had lest you should make me lose it.

" I decided that if I were indeed brooding in a retired life over a trifle, it was time to refer the matter to some one whose life was not retired, and who was better able than I to judge. I gave the whole matter to Hon. Mr. Dane. He made inquiries among the publishers, without using your name, or in any way bringing you in question; and as the result of his investigations, he reports ten per cent. on the retail price as the very lowest paid to the author. One publisher told him that they considered a book that was not worth to its author ten per cent., was not worth publishing.

" How, then, could I avoid the conclusion that you have been paying me all these years from one fourth to one third less than the lowest market price? For, notwithstanding the fixed sum was to avoid a change, change has not been avoided. When a book was published whose retail price was one dollar and fifty cents, the author's part went down to ten cents. That is, the author's price was fixed against a rise, but flexible toward a fall.

" Is not this enough to explain my ' change of sentiment' and my ' sudden dissatisfaction ?'

" Mr. Hunt, I cannot talk of this. I have suffered a loss that money cannot measure, nor words express. The writing of this letter is the most painful work my pen has ever done. My faith in you was perfect, and my friendship boundless, and it has all come to this.

" I was thoroughly identified with you. I counted your prosperity mine. Not a word of praise or censure was passed upon you that I did not feel.

Had your needs demanded it, I would gladly have offered twice, and thrice, and four times any reduction, and have reckoned it only pleasure.

"If I have failed to make anything clear, you can refer to Mr. Dane. No one but himself knows anything about it ; but how can it be kept longer ? And yet how can it be told ? "

When Mr. Hunt rendered my account, and paid my money to Mr. Dane, I found that they had allowed ten per cent. on the new book, " Rights of Men."

Mr. Hunt did not reply to my letter, but sought an interview with Mr. Dane, of which the latter gives the following account : —

"Athens, *March 2d*, 1768.

"I have had a long talk with Mr. Hunt ; longer than I can write. He asked me at first what you wished ; said he had a long letter from you, referring him to me, etc. I told him that it seemed to you, as it did to me, strange that, while almost any author was receiving ten per cent. on sales, you were allowed much less, and that was what had not been explained. He expressed all through the greatest regard for you, and surprise that you should have so little confidence in him. I told him I should be very glad to be able to assure you that he had done everything toward you that his confidential relations required, and that I felt sure it was best, in every business point of view, that he should continue your publisher.

"He said your books are published more expensively than most books; that a great deal has been always expended for advertising; that it costs, for instance, $1,000 for one page of the 'Adriatic,' —— copies being printed; that they employ one man at a yearly salary of —— dollars to attend to having their books properly noticed in the papers; that all the machinery for a large sale is expensive; that they make forty per cent. discount to the trade — more on large orders; that Mr. Somebody makes estimates of the actual cost of books published, and submits them to him, and did so with yours, and so a fair price was fixed; that you have made more out of the books than the publishers, and that they could not and cannot afford to pay more than what has been allowed; and upon my suggestion that more had been allowed on 'The Rights of Men,' he said that was a thin book, and took but little paper, and so cost less. He says others will pay you much more for a single work in order to get you, but thinks the style, etc., would not be satisfactory, etc. In short, Mr. H. claims that in all respects, they have done their best as publishers and friends for your reputation and pecuniary interests in the long run.

" Mr. H. said he was sorry you did not call as he suggested, and talk about the matter ; that he should never cease to be your friend — ' I wish you would tell her so ; ' that in your letter you had almost charged him with dishonesty, which certainly you could not mean, etc. Upon my inquiry, he said they made less on the books at the present high prices, but he gave me no special estimates. He said he had arranged with other authors at a specified price per copy, but did not tell me what price. As the interview was at his request, I had no demands to make, and could do little but hear him. I told him I should write you to-day, placing the matter before you as he presented it; that I could not, without inquiry, say to you that I was or was not satisfied that all was right, but should be very glad to see your pleasant relations continue ; and so it ended."

This explanation was not satisfactory. If my books were published more expensively than most books, Mr. Hunt should have told me before. When the first one was to be published, he asked what style I should like, and suggested that of the " City Curate." I preferred " Sir Thomas Browne." He made no objection, nor even hinted that it was more expensive than the other. He wrote to me, " It will be a beauty, and look like ' Sir Thomas Browne,'

in its red waistcoat." And again : "I am glad you
like the costume into which we put your first-born."
The following books were simply published in uniform style with the first, and nothing was ever said
about it between us. As to the cost of advertising,
why should it cost him more to advertise than it
did other publishers, or more to advertise me than
other writers ? What, again, had I to do with the
cost of the machinery for large sales, or with the
rate of discount, unless they were gotten up and
arranged solely or chiefly on my account ? In
that case I must indeed have been disastrous to
my publishers, for I cannot think my sales have
been exceptionably large. The reason alleged for
the increased price allowed on " Rights of Men,"
seemed trivial. True, it was but a thin book, and
took but little paper, and so cost less. But it was
not so thin a book as " Holidays," on which they
allowed me but ten cents, while on " Rights of
Men," accounted for after I had begun to look into
the matter, they allowed fifteen cents. Yet both
books were sold at the same retail price, — one dollar and fifty cents. " Rights of Men " was one
hundred and forty-four pages thinner than " Winter Work," one hundred and twenty-three pages
thinner than " Cotton-picking," ninety-eight pages
thinner than " Old Miasmas." Those books were
sold at a retail price of two dollars, while this was

one dollar and a half. On those books they allowed me seven and a half per cent., while on this they allowed me ten per cent.

But " Old Miasmas " is one hundred and fifty-one pages thinner than " City Lights ; " " Cotton-picking " is one hundred and twenty-six pages thinner than " City Lights." All three of the books are sold at the same retail price, — two dollars. And on all three I was allowed but seven and a half per cent. That is, while all goes smoothly, a thinness of one hundred and fifty-one pages is of no account. It neither makes the price of a book less to the buyer, nor the pay of a book greater to the author. But when ripples begin to rise, a thinness of ninety-eight pages makes the buyer's price less by fifty cents, and the author's pay greater by one-fourth. Thinness, thou art a jewel!

One thing more : as these books are published in uniform style, if they are published more expensively than most books, they must have been so published in the beginning. Therefore the relative pay of the author should then have been less. But the first contract is made out according to the usual custom, at ten per cent. on the retail price. When the author was unknown and the sale uncertain, he received ten per cent. After he became known, and the risk, one would suppose, must have been diminished, he went down to six and two-thirds per cent. Great is the mystery of publishing!

Thinking it possible that smallness of sales might have something to do with it, I wrote to Mr. Dane :—

"I can't tell a lie, pa.   I wish I was satisfied, but I am not.   If Mr. Hunt had said this to me in the first place, I dare say I should have been.   The best light is this : that I asked him a question to which, for three months, he made no reply.   You asked it, and he answered at once.   This, however, is a slight matter.   I can talk about it, and scold him for it, and, without ever forgiving him, live on in perfect good-humor.   It is a surface matter, and if this is all it is nothing.

"But I cannot thoroughly feel that this is all, and I cannot be the same without feeling so.   Mr. Jackson knew the style of the book, so did Mr. Campton, and they knew the expenses of printing; and if Mr. Hunt had so much regard for me as he thinks he had, why did he let me go on making myself wretched for weeks, when an hour's time would have set everything at rest?   He who really regards me, will regard my whims as well as my wants.   And this was not a whim, either ; it was a sensible and natural question.   Mr. Hunt is mistaken in supposing I did not mean what I seemed to mean.   I did mean just that.   If I had meant less, I should have felt less.   I am not a simpleton to break my heart over a difference of opinion. . . .

"I do not think it necessary to apply to any others than Marsh & Merriman, and Mr. Campton. If they think everything is as it should be, then be it resolved that it is. Enough testimony is as good as a feast. Why should others pay me more for a single work in order to get me? Can they afford to pay more than he? But there is no good in talking upon uncertainties. When we have found out any actual data, we can cipher on interminably. I trust you are pleased with the prospect. I do not think it is of any use to stop here, because inwardly I am no more content than I was when I began — not so much, in fact. I am at one of those places where it is easier to go forward than backward. Indeed, from this point it is impossible to go back to where I was when I started.

"Having slept over it, it occurs to me to say that I think you better see Mr. Campton and perhaps no one else. . . . . I am afraid it will somehow get out."

Mr. Dane took my accounts to Mr. Campton and laid the facts before him, making thus the matter personal for the first time. He reported: —

"I have had a long talk with Mr. Campton, and stated to him all that Mr. Hunt said as reasons for his course, as well as what the sales had been, etc. He says your books are not within his — Murray & Elder's — usual line of publication, but he

knows all about them. He says nobody would ask
you to receive less than ten per cent. on the retail
price, and any publisher in Athens will give you
more for anything you may offer, and that now you
ought to receive for all past sales at that rate on all
the books, and that you would be entitled to that
even on a book where only two thousand copies sold.

" Mr. Campton measured and counted the pages,
etc., in your books, and figured the cost and all the
items. At outside present prices it costs to compose
and stereotype such a book, $1.25 a page, or $500
for 400 pages. That is the whole outlay for the
plates ready to print. After that, the books cost,
all told, say 52 cents per copy.

" The publisher receives, including what he retails and gives away, an average of $1.20 per copy
on the whole editions.

"Such books of 400 pages cost each copy : —

Paper and press-work,	.	.	. .24
Binding,	. . . .	.	. .23
Stereotype plates, $500,			
10,000 copies, each, .	.	.	. .05
			.52

Retail price,	. . .	.	. $ 2.00
40 per cent. off,	. .	.	. .80
			$1.20
			.52
			.68

Of which the publisher has   .   .   .53

The author 15

" Old Miasmas " has only 310 pages, and so costs less by 25 per cent. Mr. C. says the books can be made at 15 per cent. less than these estimates, but he wanted to keep within bounds. . . . . The advertising, etc., are part of the usual machinery of all publishers. He says B. & H., so far from making unusual discounts to the trade, have recently published a list prescribing so little discounts that ' the trade ' are offended."

I also directed Mr. Dane to write to some of the Corinthian publishers to ascertain their custom. He wrote to Pearville & Co., and received the following reply on March 20 : —

" DEAR SIR, — In reply to your favor of 18th, beg to say that, in the absence of any agreement, we should pay to the author 10 per cent. on the retail price for all copies sold. This on $2.00 would give the author 20 cts. ; and 1.50, 15 cts. per copy.

" Very respectfully,   B. PEARVILLE & Co."

My confidence in Mr. Hunt was lost, and I was too much disheartened to do anything more except to close my connection with the firm, so far as I could. I wrote to Mr. Dane : —

4

"Do not *you* be disturbed by this unhappy complication. If you do, I shall be *désesperé* indeed. There is nothing to be done between Mr. Hunt and me. There is nothing between us worth preserving. . . . . The case has been presented to him. He is not inclined to do anything, and I certainly cannot press him. Either he feels that he is right or that he is wrong. If the former, any proceedings on my part will only bring on active antagonism. If the latter, the consciousness of it is penalty severe enough to atone for all. Moreover, so far as I am concerned, no money could make amends for what it would cost me ; and in fact, having lost so much, I think I rather enjoy losing the money too. . . I would not see Mr. Hunt any more. Let it all go."

V.

SKIRMISHING.

MR. BRUMMELL had written me, some time before, a letter on some business matter connected with his magazine, the " Buddhist," asking, I think, for a contribution. Near the last of March I wrote to him saying that I wished to have my editorial name removed from the covers of the " Buddhist," not from any dissatisfaction with its management, but from other causes ; that if for any reason it might be awkward for him to do it now, I would not press the matter, but wait his convenience.

I had no quarrel with Mr. Brummell. My acquaintance with him was very slight. I did not suppose he knew anything of my dealings with Mr. Hunt, and I made no reference to them.

A few days after, I chanced to see that my name, with those of the other editors, had already, for the last two numbers, been removed from the covers of the " Buddhist," and I wrote to Mr. Brummell again, saying that, if I had discovered that fact sooner, I should not of course have written as I did.

He replied on the 31st of March : —

" I have been much away from my desk this month. During an absence your letter — with an inclosure or two — came. Before I could reply I was again called away, and, just returning, I receive your note of yesterday.

" I wrote to you in the first place because I thought you really took an interest in the ' B.' as well as accepted its annual pecuniary recognition of your association with it, and because, since the completion of the first volume, you had contributed but very sparingly to its pages, — had almost ceased even to send me good advice and better criticism.

" I did not consider that you had broken off relations with our house *in toto,* just because you fancied another strong box more secure than ours, or wished to try whether the *parvenu* hawkers and peddlers of books could make the future of your literary life more pleasant and profitable than your past had proved by following the established routine of regular publishing. I should have thought that I was doing you an injustice had I allowed myself to fancy that, because you wanted to try a promising experiment, you and ourselves were not to [be] considered as ' on terms ' any more. Was I wrong?

" But, beyond this, I thought that if any difference of opinion were to arise as to the proper earnings to be expected from your books, there could be no question as to the return made by the ' B.' for the dozen or fifteen articles which you had contributed to it, and that as you had sent but two papers to the volume of 1767 and none for that of 1768, there could be no *faux pas* in asking you to supply something. Again — was I wrong ?

" A word as to the matter of names. It was my intention to have no editorial names on the new cover, as so much correspondence has been inflicted on ' the trio,' and as so many subscriptions have been sent to one or the other of them personally ; but by some blunder at the office, the names crept on twice before I could lay them quite.

" Am I to understand that with the withdrawal of your name from the cover of the ' B.' you desire that your relations with Maga shall cease, and the allowance heretofore made in return for your name — and for your contributions, which were originally expected to be monthly or when desired — shall no longer be passed to your credit ? "

M. N. TO MR. BRUMMELL.

" Your letter of March 31 is before me. If you will be so good as to refer to my letter to which yours is a reply, I think you will find a declaration to the effect that my wish to leave the magazine was not founded on any dissatisfaction connected with it. I certainly meant to guard against the possibility of any such supposition on your part. That I failed to do so, I must beg you to attribute to inability and not to disinclination or indifference.

" Nor did your previous letter give me the faintest shadow of offense. I was never otherwise than gratified whenever you asked me to write. When you say 'your contributions, which were originally expected to be monthly or when desired,' do you mean to intimate that there was an agreement between us to that effect? If so, permit me to say that such an agreement never existed. Mr. Hunt came to me in Zoar with a request for service and an offer of salary, which I felt obliged to refuse. He then offered me $500 per year for the use of my name as one of the editors and for such service as I chose to give the magazine. He said they should be glad to have me write every month, but I should be left absolutely free not to write at all. I thought the sum altogether too great for what I should be able to do; and it was with the utmost reluctance, and only after much urgency,— and because it was Mr. Hunt who urged it, — that I consented to the arrangement. I made no promises, but I determined in my own mind that I would send something every month; and I satisfied my editorial conscience by carefully reading every number as it came out, and noting its points, as you perhaps have some-

times found to your sorrow, or at least fatigue. I
did this for a long time. Every gap in the earlier
numbers is owing to a story rejected or delayed by
you, not to any failure on my part to send you a
story. When I found that a paper would lie two
or three months in your hands, I thought it was because you had so much better things to print, and
I considered that I was doing you a kindness by not
sending so frequently; and therefore, whenever you
did ask me to write, I took it as a compliment, and
was always pleased. You cannot speak more dis-
paragingly than I think of my actual services on
the ' Buddhist,' but I could wish that your opinion had found an earlier expression. Permit me
distinctly to say that, until the reception of your
last letter, my relations towards you in connection
with the magazine were always agreeable; while
my original scruples regarding the money value of
such an editorial arrangement were long ago set at
rest in the most conclusive manner by other publishers.

" I do wish you to understand that I.desire my
relations with the magazine shall cease at the earliest possible moment.

" That part of your letter which refers to my
reasons for breaking my connection with your
house, it is impossible for me to characterize, and
equally impossible for me to reply to."

MR. BRUMMELL TO M. N., APRIL 4.

" I have your letter of the 1st instant, and I thank you for it.

" May I correct the slight misunderstanding of my position which I fancy I detect in your reply, and for which I am doubtless responsible by reason of some ineffectiveness in my way of ‘ putting things.’

" My notion was, that if your relation with the ‘ B.’ had been agreeable, and your work satisfactorily paid, I should be sorry to lose you as helper and adviser, because you felt that you could publish elsewhere and otherwise to better advantage. Pray consider that you and I have only been in communication in regard to this magazine ; of the precise manner and nature of your dealing with our senior partner in other matters, I, of course, can know nothing. I can only receive the results.

" I had understood, on taking up the plan prepared for the ‘ B.,’ that its ostensible editors were to be *regular* contributors, — supplying for its pages articles whenever wanted, even as often as monthly.

" If I misapprehended the agreement with yourself, you must excuse me, and acquit me of intentionally overstraining it. I did use your articles slowly, for the reason, on the one hand, that I seldom had by me more than one at a time, and could not exactly count upon the receipt of another ; and, on the other hand, because I knew you to be busy on other things, and hesitated to take from you time which you might prefer to use differently, thinking that when you were moved to write, you would do so.

" Believe me, your letters of suggestion were always welcome, and would still be so. If anything in my last note — which was somewhat hurried — seemed to be cast in the form of a reflection upon you, I hope that you will consider that I did not so intend it.

" I have neither the right nor the desire to impugn your reasons for seeking another channel of communicating with the public than such as B. and H. have been able to afford, and I do not think I implied anything to the contrary. It is for you to make the best market of your writings that you can ; and although I may, as well as any other publisher, have my own view of what you should do, and what should be done for you, I am most far from wishing you to accept my view unconvinced, and I do not even offer it therefore.

" I honestly and earnestly wish you as thorough success as you can desire ; and I hope that after you have put other publishers to the *real test*, — not of telling you what their brethren ought to do, but of themselves doing what they say should be done, —

you will find as complete satisfaction from the general average of your next *five or six* years, as I am inclined to think you might derive from a consideration of a similar period just ending.

"Sincerely yours,

"H. M. BRUMMELL."

Solomon, in the enthusiasm of his love for his little sister, conjures up quaint fancies to embody his ardent longings to lavish gifts upon her. "If she be a wall, we will build upon her a palace of silver; and if she be a door, we will inclose her with boards of cedar." So, if this correspondence with Mr. Brummell were the Sacred Scriptures, one would express his admiration by writing a commentary upon it. His especial appreciation would be given to the childlike innocence with which Mr. Brummell darts out of his path in pursuit of chimerical beetles, while admonishing *me* to remember that we are concerned with but a single bug. Nor would he refuse the meed of one melodious tear to the *naïveté* with which this complete letter-writer, in his first epistle, lays bare the mercenary motives of his correspondent, and, in the second, calmly affirms, as a corollary to his propositions, that he knows nothing about the matter. We are all aware that men do speak unadvisedly with their lips, but the unconscious sweetness of Mr. Brummell's admission is the peculiar gift of Heaven to Mr. Brummell. The learned commentator might not be able to throw any light upon the points which are obscure to Mr. Brummell; nor can the impartial historian furnish any clew to the mystery of the "strong box," the "promising experiment," and the "parvenu hawkers and peddlers," so significantly mentioned. The present writer has no information on these points, and is inclined to believe that Mr. Brummell evolved them, as the German philosopher did the camel, from his moral consciousness.

But the question is not of sacred but profane literature, and we will not darken counsel by words without knowledge.

Until about the middle of March, this matter had not been mentioned to any one except Mr. Dane. Seeing the sea-change into something rich and strange, to which it was liable at the hands of the house of Brummell & Hunt, I thought it might be well to give my own version of it; and I spoke of it to some of those who were nearest me, and learned, as reported in a letter of April 18, to Mr. Dane: "A. was not much taken aback by the aspect of my affairs, — thinks they have only done by me as by others; if one is ' up ' to such things, he makes his bargains; if he leaves it to them, he gets theirs, such as they are. A. has done just as I did, never said anything about it, and they pay

what they choose. What they choose is twelve
and a half cents on a dollar and a half book, and
ten cents on a dollar and a quarter book. He says
he has made some inquiries, and supposes he could
get more elsewhere, but " O, he is rich ! " B. has
ten per cent. written contract. —————— says D. has
the same. E., of his own accord, told a friend of
mine that he did not think B. & H. were good
publishers for authors, as they advertised so little,
and had no agencies for pushing sales. I don't
agree with that, for I would much rather a book
would travel on its own merits. In fact, I have
always especially rejoiced in that attribute of B.
& H. A. says K. is shrewd and he has no
doubt *he* is well paid. But what is the use of talking about it any more ? "

MR. DANE TO M. N.

" To us mere mortals it seems as if you authors
were — as the countryman told Arthur Gilman his
lecture was — ' plaguey kinder shaller.' That . . .
you should surrender yourself at discretion to some
publisher is natural enough, but that A. should be
systematically humbugged out of his dollars, and
have the credit which I — and I presume mankind
generally — gave him for exacting so much for his
copyright as to make the price of his epistles and
things extortionate, is, as the man said of his wife's

death, ridic'lous. There is nothing in the last ' Adriatic' but —— 's poem. Tell him that the world
thinks he imposes on us by making us pay a dollar
and a half for his very thin books. We suppose he
gets their weight in gold per copyright."

VI.

A TRUCE.

HEN for a time, other events absorbed me, and the whole matter faded out of sight and thought.

Afterward, to save the trouble of repeated explanations, I determined to arrange the tragedy in compact shape, and let such of my friends as cared to know, learn it from the "original documents." Accordingly on the 27th or 28th of May, I wrote to Mr. Hunt : —

"Will you be so good as to permit me to take copies of those letters that I have sent you which resulted in breaking the connection between us? I have not my papers by me, and cannot give you the exact dates of the letters I want, but the first was sent on or about the last of December, the next, etc., etc., etc. If you desire it, I will return the letters to you, or if you prefer that they should not go out of your hands, and will say when and where I can see them, I shall be happy to suit your convenience."

Mr. Hunt did not reply to this letter directly, but sought an interview with Mr. Dane.

MR. DANE TO M. N.

" Mr. Hunt has been at my office an hour, talking of you, etc. He at first said you had written him for copies of your letters ; that he is taking account of stock and could not possibly have them copied at present, and wished, if I were writing you, that I would say so. I said, why not inclose the letters to M. N., and ask her to return them if you want them. He said he would. He seems worried about the matter, and said, ' If I only could know what M. N. wants, I would do anything to satisfy her.' I said, ' I have done all I could to prevent a final breach between you. From all I could learn, I thought M. N. had not received what she was entitled to. Everybody to whom we referred expressed this opinion. Nobody suggested that less than ten per cent. was right, and you allow her six and two thirds, and seven and one half. Her conclusion was inevitable, that you had not done right, etc.' He replied with various abstractions as to how authors forgot the various expenses, etc.

" I told him you felt hurt that he did not notice your letters asking explanation. He said he wrote you to come and see him, and he would have gone to you had you suggested it. I said what I should have done, was to see you and explain the matter, and not allow it to rest so for weeks, as if it were a matter of indifference, etc. Finally I told him what I advised you, to wait for their next account, and see whether they would not, now that high prices have to some extent passed by, allow a further percentage ; and that I suggested to you to write them, or allow me to, saying that it was hoped they might make their future accounts more satisfactory. He made no reply. I mentioned that you really felt that the ' Adriatic ' was your proper avenue to the public, and had a paper now that you hardly knew what to do with. He said, ' All she has to do is to send it along.' Well, all this talk came to nothing. The only fact that at all modifies my views is, that A., B., and the rest, seem to be treated the same, and that is a surprise to me, and takes off in a measure the c—— of taking advantage of female weakness. Ahem ! "

M. N. TO MR. DANE, JUNE 1.

" Your letter came Saturday ; but *my* letters have not yet appeared from Mr. Hunt. His talk to you looks like subterfuge. I never suggested his getting the letters copied, but send them to me and I would return them, or tell me where and when I should see them, and I would wait his convenience. Again, what have I to do with the expenses of publishers ? I am not complaining that he pays small per cent., but that he, in the first place, pays less than other publishers, and secondly, pays me less than he pays other authors, and is thereby guilty of a breach of faith."

On the same day, May 29, the firm of Brummell & Hunt addressed a letter to Mr. Dane, saying, —

"We have occasion to print several volumes of M. N.'s writings, which under ordinary circumstances we should proceed to do at once. Before doing so, however, in the present posture of affairs, we have an offer to make to M. N. The dissatisfaction which she feels, and is constantly expressing toward us as her publishers, would probably lead her to prefer that her books should be in other hands. We are willing to sell the stereotyped plates and manufactured stock of her books, at a reasonable price, to any publisher with whom she may choose to arrange for their future publication.

"An early answer would be acceptable, as in the event of our retaining the books, we wish to proceed with the manufacture."

MR. DANE TO M. N., JUNE 1, 1768.

"The breezes from B. & H. are very fluctuating. The same day in which Mr. H. came and had the long talk which I reported to you, the firm seem to have written the inclosed, which I did not get till this morning.

"If you don't do anything for a month nothing

in particular will happen.   Still, you want the books
in the market, and perhaps somebody will take them
off B. & H.'s hands and do as well. . . . .

"I am somewhat inclined to say to them that we
will take all the stereotype plates, and all the books
on hand of them, at the appraisal of fair men.   And
the same men shall adjust all claims for the past
copyrights.

"I am surprised at this blunt note, after Mr. H.'s
amiable conversation.   If we are going to have a
settlement, let us open the past and make them
refer the whole thing; let them give up everything
and adjust the balance as fair men shall say is
right." . . . .

But the note of the firm did not suggest any settlement of past claims; and therefore presented but
a lame and impotent conclusion to the matter.
What I wanted was indemnity for the past, not
security for the future.   If a man cheats me once,
says the proverb, it is a shame to him.   If he cheats
me twice it is a shame to me.   The information that
I was feeling and constantly expressing dissatisfaction might perhaps be classified among the " locals "
as " startling if true."   What I felt must have been
entirely a matter of inference, as it was long since
I had expressed either satisfaction or dissatisfaction;
I had been concerned in other matters.   My note

to Mr. Hunt contained no emotional expressions whatever. But as I had had my full share of sentimentalizing, it was no more than fair that Messrs. B. & H. should have their turn at it.

Their course seemed to me mere child's play, and not the play of good children either; which must serve as excuse for the following reply sent to Mr. Dane : —

" Your letter came this morning. Messrs. Brummell & Hunt have improved even on Mr. Brummell. His felicitous, original idea was only that I was impelled by a desire to have recourse to the " parvenu hawkers and peddlers of books." The combined wisdom of the firm seems to point to my becoming a parvenu hawker and peddler myself. Their fine instinct has doubtless divined my long-cherished dream of setting up a book-stall beside the orange-woman in the neighboring corner of the Common.[1] Pray present my compliments to Messrs. Brummell & Hunt, and say to them with many thanks, that as this new career could hardly be said to open brilliantly with an array of obsolete and obsolescent volumes, I do not propose to enter upon

[1] A " Common " is a tract of ground which belongs not to individuals but to the public. Probably the bookstore referred to was on the outskirts of the city, and the " Common " was the land as yet unappropriated by builders, and on which, doubtless, sheep and cows grazed undisturbed. — *Note by Editor.*

it until some new work appears, when I shall crave
their blessing not their books.

"Do not be at the trouble of transmitting this
message. Send the letter down bodily, and let it
whistle itself."

On Monday, the 1st of June, one of my friends,
Rev. Mr. Hayes, having gone to Mr. Hunt with
the olive-branch in his hand, but without my knowledge, and been completely won over by his amiable
bearing, came to me, and begged me, if only out
of regard to himself, to have an interview with Mr.
Hunt. I had been familiar for several years with
Mr. Hunt's gifts and graces, and knew that, though
they were charming for social intercourse, they
were not easily reducible to two and a half, still less
to three and one-third per cent. But, as Mr. Hayes
begged me by his friendship; as, regarding Mr.
Hunt, everything which I had cared to save was
lost, and as I wanted my letters, which, though
promised, did not come, I consented, so far as to
give Mr. Hayes permission to say to Mr. Hunt that
if he chose to come to my house to bring my letters,
I would be at home on Thursday, the 4th of June.

M. N. TO MR. DANE.

"Mr. Hunt is coming down on Thursday to bring
me my letters. I think it a foolish and useless, as

it is a most disagreeable thing; foolish, simply because useless; but I have agreed to it so far as to say that I should be at home. The talk will amount to nothing because I cannot talk. He will have it all his own way, because it is a subject on which he is informed and I am not. And then, talk is never tangible. I want something that you can keep hold of. But at any rate, I shall get my letters. It is impossible to refer it to arbitrators, because the worst part of my trouble was not of such sort as could come before them. I will never permit the matter to go before arbitrators unless it comes to be a case of honor. That is, I will not do it for the sake of what money I might get."

M. N. TO MR. DANE.

"Mr. Hunt came down on Thursday, as I expected. He was in some sort my guest, and we met amicably, and parted *friendlily.* The most important development of his visit was, that [he says] he did, in the early stages of the affair, send me just such a letter as I told him he should have sent, — a letter written, as he says, by his own hand, because he would not have his clerk mixed up in it; written with great pain, and the only letter he has written since his hand has been so lame, except one to Dickens.[1] In this, he assured me that it was all

[1] "The dickens!" is an exclamation of playful surprise. Probably

right, that he had the figures to show me so, notwithstanding appearances; and begged me to let
him come to Zoar and do so. This, without any
other explanation, would have quite satisfied me in
the beginning; but this letter I never received. Of
course, however, I receive his assertion that such a
letter was written, and I make the best use I can
of it. He assured me, in the most solemn manner,
that he has done by me as he has done by A., B.,
and the others; and that he has always done what
he thought the best thing and most to my advantage. Now, when a man tells me that, I can have
nothing more to say to him. H. has a greater percentage because his books have never been printed
but once, and that when work was cheaper, and so
they pay him at the old prices. But I will go into
particulars more fully when I see you. I suppose
it is pretty much the same as you have heard yourself. . . . . He admitted that he did not wonder
at my course, seeing I had not received his letter,
yet seemed to think I should have had more confidence in him; had always supposed *I* should stand
by him, though the heavens fell. The heavens did
not fall, though I sometimes think a part of the sky
is not there. I told him that I had no intention to

the word as here used, is a corruption of this phrase, and was merely
a strong way of expressing, on Mr. Hunt's part, that he had written
no other letter at all. But after so great a lapse of time it is impossible to get at the exact truth. — *Note by Editor.*

meddle with the past; agreed that they should go on with their books as if nothing had happened, and desired him, whatever course I might take in the future, to believe me not unfriendly toward himself, but that the developments of this trouble had made it impossible for me at once to resume my old place. But I don't think he minded that.

"Now you see . . . . we are at peace. I do not deceive myself. It is not a very rapturous sort of peace. The relations between us are but a thin, meagre, unsubstantial substitute for those that formerly existed; but they are better than war — and they are truer than the old ones, — and truth is better than falsehood, however agreeable the falsehood be. I do not mean that on either side there was any intentional falsehood, but that there was a sort of glamour which is now removed.

"Now, if any one ever speaks to you of this, say, as I shall, that there was a misunderstanding, but that it is removed.

"I hope that you will not disapprove of what I have done; or perhaps, rather, of what I have not done, for my action has been chiefly a negative. I have simply let things be, in form, which I have always meant to do in substance. He assures me that it is all right, and I cannot stand up and dispute his word."

Mr. Hunt, during this interview, insisted that at the time he made the change from ten per cent. to fifteen cents, he had a long talk with me and fully explained the reason. I insisted that he never had done so. I admitted that he had announced that he was going to make the change on account of the fluctuations in the prices of things, and the consequent uncertainties. It was all I wanted, and more. If he had said nothing I should have been just as well satisfied, I had so much faith in him. A positive assurance generally carries it over a negative. Still, if a man asserted that he had offered himself to a girl, her negative assertion that he never had, would, of itself, be entitled to as much credence as his positive one, supposing the character of both to be equal. If the man were in the habit of offering himself to girls, while the girl had never had another lover, her negative would surely outweigh his positive. Mr. Hunt had dealings with many authors. He was my only publisher, and he was more likely to be mistaken in this than I. He might have intended to make the explanation, or might have made it to some one else; but an explanation made to me, it is next to impossible I should have forgotten.

Really, the matter was not of importance, because if he had made it then it would have answered every purpose. If I could have been made to see

at one time, that seven and a half equals ten, I
could have been made to see it at another.

Here the controversy seemed to have come to a
natural and pacific conclusion, and I began to take
up the burden of life again, saying only, it might
have been different perhaps, but then it might not.
I cannot affirm that I was entirely satisfied about the
missing letter. Letters never are lost in our climate.
We often wish they would be. There are dozens
in this correspondence, nothing in whose life would
have become them like the leaving it. But they
all went straight as an arrow to the mark, and now,
like Burns' sonsie, smirking, dear-bought Bess,

> "They stare their daddy in the face;
> Enough of aught ye like, but grace."

On the 24th of February, Mr. Hunt seemed first
to have awakened to the fact that there was any
cloud in the sky, and begged me in all kindness to
tell him the ground of my sudden dissatisfaction.
Of course, the missing letter could not have been
written before that time. After I replied to him,
alleging the grounds of my sudden dissatisfaction, he
replied by calling on Mr. Dane, as Mr. Dane's letter to me shows. I was not only unable to find any
place where Mr. Hunt's explanatory letter might
have been missing, but I could not find a place
where it could have come in.

But I let that pass. There seemed to be nothing

more to do, and if there had been, I was too tired to do it. I thought the affair, like David's destructions, had come to a perpetual end, which, if not absolutely satisfactory, was at least relatively so. There are very few kinds of peace which are not better than war. I was not sure I had done the wisest thing, and as I wrote to Mr. Dane in review of it, " to speak the truth in love, I don't much care. That is, the whole affair had become so utterly tiresome to me that I long ago grew indifferent to it. How the business part of it should be settled, I little cared. What I really had at stake, is lost."

VII.

RENEWAL OF HOSTILITIES.

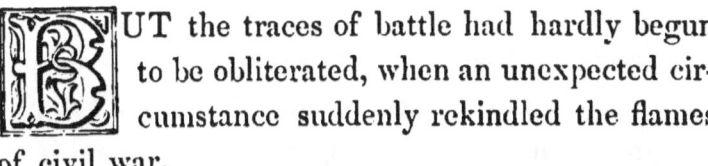UT the traces of battle had hardly begun to be obliterated, when an unexpected circumstance suddenly rekindled the flames of civil war.

My sorrow's crown of sorrow had been that so bewailed in the lamentations of the prophet, that there was no sorrow like unto my sorrow; but by the chance of a word, without any revelation on my part, I discovered that a friend of mine was, and had been for some months, going through the same pleasant process which I had been enjoying. The similarity of operation was, in certain respects, remarkable. No accounts had been rendered for years, the author trusting entirely in the friendship of his publishers; so that of course there were no papers to be produced. But there was the same change from a still higher percentage to a lower fixed sum; the same assertion on the one side, of a full explanation made and accepted, which explanation was totally denied on the other; and the same declaration of regard for the author himself. The case was more aggravated than mine, not only because the author in question had been of an immeasurably higher standing than I, but also because he was dead, and the apparent exactions were made upon those who were dearest to him in life, and who were dependent upon the fruits of his genius. So then, mine was no longer an isolated case, but part of a regular system. How many of the writers who had received reduced pay had really and intelligently agreed to it, and how many had found it, like greatness, thrust upon them, and had accepted it on the representation of its being universal, rather than make an ado and appear churlish ? My friend certainly denied that any explanation had been made, or even that any notice of the change had been given her beforehand, and she rebelled against the change as soon as she did know it. Now, it is hard fighting just your own battles, since no matter how right you may deem your cause for quarrel, still it *is* a quarrel, and a mere personal altercation has always something in it petty and demeaning; but if you can fight for somebody else, you mount at once to higher ground and gain the vantage. It came to me at once, as clear as light, that I was doing exactly what Messrs. Brummell & Hunt had wisely counted on our all doing, in case we did anything; that is, fretting a little, perhaps, but eventually letting it all drop, silenced if not convinced. Was it not the height of presumption for any one son of Jesse to come out with a sling and a stone against this Goliath of the publishers? Would it not be ridiculous to charge with injustice this house, whose praise for liberality is in all the churches? Of course in discussing the details of the business, the author would have to go entirely out of his sphere, while the house would be perfectly at home. Still I thought if I could not be a stone in the forehead of my giant, I could be a thorn in his side.[1] If he were honorable and just in his dealings, no charge could harm him. If he were unjust, no reputation could save him. If his gains were well-gotten, investigation would only establish him more firmly in his right way. If they were ill-gotten, it might be possible to prevent his repose in enjoying them, if he could not be induced to give them up, and he might thus be deterred from further ravage upon the unwary. The best way to serve the general weal was to take up my own relinquished cause. I accordingly once more put my hand to the plough, resolved not to look back till I had drawn a straight furrow through my pleasant fields.

While I was reflecting upon total depravity, pre-

---

[1] The Editor trusts that it is not necessary for him to point out to his youthful readers that this spirit is not presented to them for an ensample.

paratory to a renewal of hostilities — there may be a sudden transition from metaphor to metaphor, but let us all be thankful if nothing more than rhetoric becomes demoralized, — the following note came from Mr. Dane, to whom I had communicated the tale of Mrs. ——'s fancied or real woes, August 10.

" Whether those five postage-stamps pasted firmly on the first page of your note were intended as a birth-day present, instead of the Family Bible which I had some reason to think I might receive about this time, or as payment of arrears for services *in re* M. N. *vs.* B. & H., I do not know. I might add, — but will not for fear of being sarcastical, — that it is far more than I expected either way, and that such munificence is more illustrative of the generosity of the giver than of the deserts of the humble recipient.

" And now I have a profound secret to impart to you and your nine particular friends. I have kept it two days, and had some thoughts of never telling you, but since you claim the relation of client, I am not at liberty to humbug you, — pardon the inelegance, — as I cheerfully would do were you only a dear female friend. Well, Mr. Edwards called Saturday, and saying to him that I spoke, as St. Paul always speaks to you when you don't agree with him, by permission and not by my own inspira-

tion, I renewed our griefs ' *Jubes renovare dolorem?*'
and told him all. He, though like the rest of us, true
to his client, is evidently intimate with Mr. Hunt.
He said B. & H. are willing, and propose to Mrs.
———— that the contract which Mr. Edwards has
made with them, that she should receive twelve
cents a volume on the sales, shall be given up, and
that they will refer to two gentlemen of satisfactory
character the matter of her future percentage. . . .

" Then with that admirable frankness which is so
natural to me, I said to Mr. Edwards that Mr. Hunt
had made a great mistake with you ; that you had
accepted his commercial civilities as personal regard,
and that he ought at least to keep up the standard
of his conduct to common civility in his correspondence, etc., and that it was only because you would
not follow my advice that matters were allowed to
rest ; that *my* opinion was, you had not received a
just, much less a liberal share of the profits, and
that I had urged you to propose to refer the matter
of percentage to some disinterested person, which I
thought they could not decline.

" Mr. Edwards at once said, ' Mr. Hunt shall do
that. That shall be done at once.'

" Evidently Edwards thinks he can induce Hunt
to propose that to you, and will endeavor to do so.

" Now, I thought at first I would not let you see
my hand in the matter, but that is, on reflection,

not quite fair as between man and man, — using the
word in its largest sense, embracing woman. Wherefore, pray do not call on B. & II. for any account
just now, but wait and see if they do write you, as
Edwards is sure they will, proposing to satisfy you
in this way. If they do then you must accept the
proposition, provided the past be also included, for
it is the past which made you dissatisfied. You
have not yet concluded yourself as to past or future,
so far as I know; and if the best man in the world
says you ought to have no more than has been
allowed you *I* say we ought to be satisfied. The
money I gave you ought to last longer than this.
If you want a hundred dollars send me an order on
B. & II., and I will present it and send you the
money, and that will not commit us to their percentage.

"Now I expect partly that you will be vexed at
my meddling with your affairs in this way; but fiat
justitia, etc., whoever *rue it.*"

M. N. TO MR. DANE, AUGUST 11, 1768.

"Unquestionably you *need* the Family Bible more
than the postage-stamps, which I did *not* paste on.
It must have been the dog-days that did it.

"Of course I am not vexed at your meddling,
and you only say that, as you express it, shamming.
I hate to have the thing come up again, but it may

be more effectually laid by it. One thing, though, if all the men in the world say I have had enough, it will not alter my relations toward Mr. Hunt. That is, if he proves conclusively that his terms have been just and liberal, I shall still think that his course toward me since I began to make inquiries has been ungentleman-like, unfriendly, and calculated to arouse instead of allay suspicion, and that Mr. Brummell was grossly impolite. So, after all, what will be settled by a reference? Nothing but the money affair, which indeed, as it involves justice, is much, but as it does not involve regard, is little. However, integrity is all the world wide from and more than good manners. I will not send for any account or money either. I let a friend have my money for a few months to accommodate him, so that I am penniless again; but I can borrow plenty, and Fred and Fritz are as good as new milch cows in a house. Why I am in such a hurry to write is, that I have a letter from Hyperion this morning, in which he seemed to think you would be the proper person to act for Mrs. ———, rather than Sir Matthew Hale, who is occupied with the weightier matters of the law. Now I do not want you to act for her. It would look as if you made it a personal matter; as if we were persecuting Mr. Hunt, which is not true. Mrs. ———'s affair is as entirely different from mine as if I did not know her at all.

. . . . I will let you know as soon as I hear from Mr. Hunt. What day did you see Mr. Edwards? I had a letter yesterday from Smilex conjuring me to write for the 'Heretic,' and offering me good pay, but not stating what. I have not answered it yet. I am in a strait betwixt two, not to say half a dozen. . . . . If B. & H. send to me, how will it do for you to come down ? I will pay your fare, and you can board round ! "

MR. DANE TO M. N., AUGUST 14.

" How foolish in you to expect Mr. Hunt to make you any such proposition. He never will, though Mr. Edwards seems sure he will. What do you care when he called ? Call it the day before I wrote last. . . . .

" One little matter of business. You request me not to act for Mrs. ———. If you expect me not only to transact your business, but also not to transact any for anybody else, you will see the necessity of your charging yourself with the support of my family, largely dependent on my business income for their thrice daily bread. . . . .

" As to writing for ' The Heretic,' you doubtless desire my opinion, though diffidence or something prevents your saying so. If it was not a dream of yours that they offered you a million, tell them you will accept that proposition. If you don't publish something soon, I have no doubt you will have a congestion of the intellect.

"The ' Respectability ' is nothing compared with ' The Heretic.' As you write under your own signature you will not be responsible for the rest of the paper. You want the pay, — to lend to your friends, who will increase, as your capacity to lend is known to increase.

" And now farewell ; and don't expect any such letter from Hunt, though he may probably write something."

MR. DANE TO M. N., AUGUST 21.

" What did you send Mrs. ———'s letter to me for, if you don't want me to have anything to do with her affairs? Still, *homo sum*, I am somewhat of a man, and although forbidden to advise Mrs. ———, am interested in general history.

" You did not promise to tell me how you disburse your money ; and what good can it do for me to know that you have thrown it into the sea, or laid it up where moths and rust do not corrupt? You are not fit to make loans as matter of business, as perhaps I intimated to you soon after our chase after that hundred dollars which was in your basket. I hope you will help all you can. There is no better use for money, when one has plenty of it, and I trust your efforts in behalf of young doctors and things will be sanctified to their and your everlasting good.

" As to sending for B. & H.'s account, I have no expectation that they will take any notice of Mr. Edwards' advice, or make you any proposition. . .

" The question is, do you mean to take just what they say, or do you propose to insist on more than the fifteen cents per copy ?

" As you don't and won't take my advice and make them do right, you must decide what you *will* do."

M. N. TO MR. DANE, AUGUST 22.

" Why I sent you the letters, was because I was interested in the case, and what I am interested in it is proper you should be likewise. All is, I don't want you to loom up as her advocate ; but if you know the circumstances you may perhaps, in a quiet way, keep her from falling into a ditch. And so you being wise as a serpent, and I harmless as a dove, we may perhaps circumvent those wicked and unprofitable servants. . . . . .

" Moreover, as you have already observed, the case does bear directly on mine. Not only do they profess themselves willing to compromise with Mrs. —— on ten per cent., but in this letter ' they say ' that ' even B. now has only ten per cent.' (from which I infer that he has had more). But

Mr. Hunt, in this house, told me that they did by me just as they did by B.

"Now I do not feel disposed to let the past go. They have not done by me as they have done by others. Why would it not do for you to make the proposal to them since they do not make it? I would just as soon make it, if you say so. Perhaps it would come best from me in a letter to be delivered by you. I have no sensitiveness whatever about it. I am as hard as steel towards them. They are so bungling that I could find it in my heart to be indignant. . . . .

" I do not propose to insist on ten per cent. to the extent of taking my books away from them, but I *am* ready to propose a reference. If they agree to it, I think it would be a good plan to find out what is the custom of other publishers, Troubadours, for instance, and a few more of the leading ones.

"I will also get one or two more of B. & H.'s authors. You see I am prepared to do now what you wished me to do long ago ; but do not plume yourself on that fact, for the timing of a thing may be as strong a test of wisdom as the doing of it. I must keep you in proper subjection at any cost.

" Mr. Heath, of the Ancient and Honorable, came down to see me, Tuesday, but I was away.

" Three hundred dollars for what I can do is more than five thousand for what I cannot. . . . .

" *Monday morning.* It has all come to me as clear as day what to do. You find out when the prices of the books went above $1.50. Until then, ten per cent. and fifteen cents were the same thing. In 1763, they had not gone up. Then cipher out from my accounts precisely how much is due me on all the books at ten per cent. Then send the papers to me and I will have Fritz *prove* your figures, Fritzes being good at 'figgers.' Then *I* will write to Mr. H., saying I have been made acquainted with Mrs. ———'s affairs, and that he offers her ten per cent. or a reference, and that I wish he would make me the same offer. You shall see the letter, and you will see that it will be very wise, and I *don't* see how he can reject, and I think he will pay the arrearage. I will tell him exactly what is due according to my thinking, and if he sees the sum all reckoned up for him, he would rather pay it than have any more fuss. Probably the reason he has not paid before is, that it was such a hard " sum " to " do." He must see that I shall be a thorn in his side as long as I live, and we, all of us, live to be eighty."

M. N. TO MR. HUNT, AS REFERRED TO IN THE PRE-
CEDING LETTER.

" On the 3d of August, I went on a visit to Mrs. ———, and there learned for the first time that her relations with you were not satisfactory to herself. Since then, she has reported to me somewhat of her proceedings, — and among other things, that Mr. Edwards says that you say that even B. now has but ten per cent. But I understood you to say the last time you were here that you did by B. just as you did by me. Also, Mr. Edwards says that you are quite willing to pay Mrs. —— ten per cent., or to refer the matter to disinterested persons for decision. I understood from you when the second contract was made, that you were going to do by all just as you proposed to do by me. I understood when you were here that you had done by all just as you have done by me. But Mr. Edwards reports you to have said that you pay B. ten per cent., and are willing to pay Mrs. —— ten per cent. C. says you pay F. ten per cent., and G. says you pay her ten per cent. Why, then, should you not pay me ten per cent.? You have paid only six and two thirds and seven and one half per cent. on a large part of the books. So long as the price of the book was $1.50, ten per cent. and fifteen cents were the same. After the price went up, they were not the same. The difference it would not be hard for you to ascertain from your books, and this difference, I believe, you ought to pay me. If you think you ought not, have you any objection to refer the mat-

ter to disinterested persons of good character and
capacity? Of course, I know that legally I have
no right to go behind a contract, and, therefore, no
legal claim upon you for additional money on those
books that are named in the contract."

COMMENTS OF MR. DANE TO M. N., SEPTEMBER 5.

" And so you have sent your letter. Much good
may it do you. My private opinion is, that you
wont get much of a reply. All the money you will
make out of the frolic is, that possibly they will
allow you ten per cent. or more on future sales.
As to the past, the woodchuck left that hole, when
you so verdantly assured Mr. H. that you had no
idea of making any claims for arrears; and any
amount of barking (pardon me, but the unity of
the figure must be maintained at any cost) will not
scare out another animal.

" Man is not a rhinoceri-hos that his skin should
not be pervious, and your arrows will rankle in the
'firm' skin of B. & H.; but business is business,
and, though a prophet spake unto them from above,
a larger, louder profit speaks to them from below.
By the way, don't consider my fees contingent on
the arrearages. Arrearages don't maintain families.
. . . . I want to see you. Perhaps you will come
over and get that money of B. & H. for arrearages.
But don't wait for that."

" It is easy to see from the altered tone of your
letters that you consider my case hopeless. Formerly you were deferent and sympathetic. Now,
wounded dignity forbids me to say what you are,
but, I repeat with Mrs. Porcupine Temper, in the
reading-book, ' Never man laughed at the woman
he loved. As long as you had the slightest remains of regard for me you could not thus make
me an object of ridicule. Happy, happy Mrs.
Granby ! '

" I wonder, however, that you should not have
taken warning from the great failure of Louis Napoleon anent Maximilian,[1] and waited till I was actually overcome before you waxed fat and kicked.
The figure may seem rude, but, besides being ap-
posite, it is Scriptural. I wish you were susceptible
to ideas. You pounce down with melancholy persistency on the fact that I assured Mr. Hunt I had
no idea of making any claims for arrearages,
which, by the way, is no fact at all. What I assured him was, that I had no intention of taking
my books out of his hands. (That is what I meant
by not meddling with the past.) Nor had I ; nor
have I now even — but never mind that. The point
is — now do squinny up your eyes and try to see
it, there's a dear, you cannot think how nice it feels

---

[1] Here the narrative seems to deviate into prophecy.—*Note by Ed.*

not to be stupid — the point is, when I told Mr.
Hunt that, or when I talked with him about it, he
assured me that he had done by others just as he
had done by me.' I had never investigated his dealings with other writers, except ———. What you
and I looked into was the way of other publishers
with their writers. Did not you yourself, violating
all the commandments at one fell swoop, say that
other writers of B. & H. sharing my misery, took
off the — the — the — kurrssee — of imposing on
unsuspecting innocence? Well, then, so I concluded my strength was to sit still, and still accordingly I sat, till I found they had not done by their
other writers as they had by me, and then up I
sprang again. Now it seems to me that I have a
right to open the case all new.

"See here — let us put it scientifically.

" PART I.

" *Unexpressed basis of operations*, B. & H. will
do as well as other publishers.

" *Ascertained fact*, They don't.

" *Result*, I fly into a rage.'

" PART II.

" *Their assurance*, They have the same rule for
all, and believe it to be the best for all, me included.

" *Result second*, I am calmed if not convinced.

"PART III.

" *Unexpected development,* They do not have the same rule for all, but make invidious distinctions, contrary to their own direct assertions, and *I* am invidiously distinguished.

" *Result,* Seven spirits more wroth than the first, and the fat in the fire.

" They have not answered my letter which I sent a week ago last Saturday. It is their way of doing business, namely, *not* doing it. I shall not write again. What I think should be done next is for you to call upon them and make a proposal of reference in form — if there is any such thing. What I wish decided is, not future percentage merely, but past percentage; whether my claim for ten per cent. on all past sales is or is not founded in or on equity. If you are present, they must make some reply. If they assent, the Troja may be comprehended in a *nuce.* If they refuse, we will consider as to the next thing to be done — but find that out first. If you don't understand this, just say over the multiplication-table two or three times, and it will clear you up like an egg-shell. The figure supposes that you are a pot of coffee.

" Your candid opinion of my letter, as compared with Mrs. ———'s, is undoubtedly just, as well as candid. She is a very fine woman, far my superior, and looks upon this affair quite as wisely as I ; but if I think the same as she does, of course it helps her.   I wish I did know how to advise her, but I don't, and you would not twit me if you did not think I was going by the board.   She is a lovely woman, and it is wicked in them to make her so much trouble.   I suppose I was born for storms, and so it is not so sacrilegious to rain and hail and thunder on me.   But if you don't roar me gently, I will change lawyers, and then what is to keep you from the work-house ?

" I had a letter to-day from Hawkers, asking me to let them publish a book for me.   They say they . . . . think they can make the results every way satisfactory.   I talked with Confucius about my letter to Mr. Hunt.   In fact, I talk with anybody now, — entertain my visitors with the correspondence.   If you don't wish to wait on Mr. Hunt with my proposal, say so.   I would invite you down here to talk it over, but there is nothing in the house to eat but a lamb's tongue and a half, and a pot of lard.   My housekeeper has disappeared, and the season is over. Even the hens have stopped laying.   A friend who came Friday and stopped till to-day, took the precaution to bring a pair of chickens with him.   I do not mean this as a hint, but as my woman is gone, I will remark that unless you are fond of fowl *à la raw*, you had better roast your chickens before you come.

"As you said nothing about the particular point in the ——— letter, I suppose your brain is as blank on the subject as mine. But I have not that inordinate love of brilliancy that I cannot open my mouth unless I expect diamonds to drop out. I am meekly content if only pebbles fall for paving-stones to feet that I love! Great applause."

MR. DANE TO M. N., SEPTEMBER 9.

"As a general rule or fact or thing, when a lawyer takes a view of the case less hopeful than the client's, and presents the difficulties, the client suspects that the lawyer is indifferent to his interests, or bribed by the other side. Anything rather than that his case is hopeless. Still the lawyer must be true; he can do no otherwise, *ruat cælum.*

" Now [here follow questions.]

" You say now *I* should propose a reference. Are you willing I should write to B. & H., and say that you have placed with me (or with R. and me, for we are partners in all law business, and have no separate names as lawyers) your claim for arrearages, with instructions to enforce them by law? If you are, I want the premier's opinion of the matter, and if we think you have a case, we will proceed. Now that you, after referring Mr. H. to me as your friend, and what has transpired under that arrangement, have had a personal interview

with him, which you announce to your friends as a
pacification, and have opened a new correspondence
with him, proposing a reference, there is embarrassment all around.   My office of friend or mediator,
they will say, is finished.   They cannot be expected
to deal with you and me both.   I think if they
do not notice your proposition, we should make no
further move, unless it is to be followed by legal
proceedings, if necessary.   There is no force or
fitness in a proposition from me, unless we have
something besides wooden guns behind it.

Now, I wish you would come and see me.   I
don't eat raw chickens, so I can't go there.   Here,
there are good victuals. . . . .   As Mrs. ———'s
case bears on yours, it concerns me no further, except to save you from conspicuous folly in your
attempts to help.   Mrs. ——— has Mr. Edwards
for her friend, adviser, and legal counsellor, and
although she is worrying his life out by constantly
twitting him of his folly, in the contract he made
as administrator, she wants no other.   He is only
skin and bone, poor man, and would die gladly,
except for fear of meeting ——— in some place
where suicide is impossible, and "twelve cents a
volume" will sound forever in his ears.

"If B. & H. do not reply to your last letter, you
may depend upon it that nothing but legal suasion
will move them.   This is not cross, though it seems
so.   I am your very amiable."

" Your letter of 29th ult., addressed to our Mr. Hunt, was duly received, and we now beg to reply on his behalf and that of the firm.

" In your letter you assume that we have but one set of terms with the various authors whose works we publish. In this you are in error. What we pay to any individual author is a matter quite between him — or her — and ourselves, and it is not our custom to make one author the criterion for another. Many elements enter into the case that would make a uniform rate impracticable. Independently of other considerations, the varying cost of manufacture caused by different styles of publication, would alone preclude such an arrangement. We must, therefore, decline to admit such an argument into the case.

" We have given our reasons in justification of our course towards you in full, and we see no occasion for repeating them here. As they were unsatisfactory to you, we offered, on May 29 last, in a letter to your attorney, Mr. Nathan Dane, to relinquish, at a fair price, the plates and stock to any publisher whom you might prefer. This offer we now respectfully renew.

" Touching arbitration, we may say that at an earlier stage of the proceedings we should have been willing to submit the matter to that test.   At present, however, we do not wish to do so."

" I am very glad you did not go to B. & H.'s, as the day after my letter to you went I received one from them, saying, ' In your letter,' etc.

" As the proceedings have been of an entirely private nature, without any cost of money, and with the outlay of but a few pages of note paper on their part, I do not see why the question of time is so important.

" What I propose now to do, is to have you, if you see no objection, send them by mail the note which I inclose to you for them.

" Legal proceedings I cannot, for a moment, think of instituting.   Even if I should gain the case, it would be at a cost altogether too great.   I think it would be far wiser for me to go on winning new laurels than to spend my energies in trying to pick up the withered twigs of last year's growth !   The figure, I perceive, has serious defects, but you don't, so we will let it pass.   I think now the whole thing would far better be suffered to remain quiet. I shall be gathering facts which will one day take shape, but I do not know what.   Knowledge, however, is always useful, and certainly one cannot move an army unless one has an army.

" So I suppose there is no need of answering your other questions.

" I think it is as well to let the books be where they are. . . . . Unless I find there is more advantage to be gained by a removal than I can see, the game would not be worth the candle.

" I feel more satisfied than I have done at any time since the trouble began. (While the child was yet alive, I fasted and wept. But now he is dead, wherefore should I fast ?) Their refusal to refer seems to put me in open seas again.

" You say you are not cross, and I know you tried hard not to be. In fact, you have been an angel of patience all through, and I mean to reward you by conducting you honorably through some difficult Hell-gate of your own. I use the term in a marine and figurative sense. . . . . From the beginning of your letter, I infer that you thought my last letter found some fault with you client-wise. I cannot recall the letter enough to know what may have given rise to the feeling, but I assure you nothing was further from the truth. And nothing can be more friendly and helpful than your whole course towards me has been. I shall never cease to hold it in grateful remembrance until you offend me, and then it will crisp up like flax in the flames, and I shall bear down on you just as heavily as if

7

you had never done me a good turn in your life. Such, alas! is human nature."

M. N. TO B. & H., SEPTEMBER 11.

" I have received your letter of the 8th inst., declining arbitration.

" I suppose, therefore, the only resource left me is the arbitration of public opinion.

" The argument which you decline to admit into the case was introduced there by Mr. Hunt. I recognize with you its disastrous effects, and applaud your prudence in excluding it.

" Regarding your offer to sell the books to another publisher, I may say that as the cream of their sale is already gone, I do not see the brilliant advantage to be derived from taking the skim milk to another publisher. I will, however, consult my board of attorneys, — pray do not suppose I limit myself to one — and beg you meanwhile, to accept my thanks for the benefit you design me.

" Will you have the goodness to send me my accounts for the last half-year."

I supposed this was the end of it, but was surprised by a letter of September 14, saying: —

" We have your letter of the 11th inst.

" We think no occasion for arbitration in the matters at issue between us need ever have arisen.

And we think, now, that a formal arbitration — as a means of settling the existing difficulties — would not prove a suitable or satisfactory method either to you or to us. We wish, however, to deal with you in a spirit of entire fairness, and we therefore propose another method, which will answer the same end in a much better way. Let us find a proper person, whose relations to both parties are such as to fit him to act as a confidential friend and adviser in the case. Let us confide the entire case, in all its bearings, to his intercession, and abide by his judgment. We have in mind a gentleman who, as we believe, would be in every way suitable and satisfactory to both, — Samuel Rogers, Esq., of this city. We understand Mr. Rogers to be a warm friend of yours, and we know him to be a just man, of sound judgment, and capable of taking a comprehensive view of the whole matter.

"If Mr. Rogers will accept the friendly office, we are quite ready to meet him in all fairness and candor, and to open our books and accounts to his inspection."

M. N. TO B. & H., SEPTEMBER 16.

"Permit me to acknowledge the reception of your letter of the 14th inst.

"I cannot, at present, give your proposal [I believe I said *proposition*, but proposal must be the right word] sufficient consideration to reply to it, but I will do so as soon as possible. Meanwhile, may I ask you to send me my accounts for the last six months? I suppose they can be made up independently of the question at issue between us.

"I most emphatically agree with you in the opinion that no occasion for arbitration need ever have arisen."

M. N. TO MR. DANE, SEPTEMBER 17.

" I thought I had pronounced my valedictory, but coming home after a few day's absence, I find the following note from B. & H. [then follows a copy of their last letter.]

" Now, this is a move which I do not understand. Why should they have declined so decidedly my proposal, and after they had received my note, why should they up and make another which, for aught I see, amounts to the same thing? I am inclined to accept the proposal, though I don't see why they should not have accepted mine. Would not Mr. Rogers be a good man?

" Isn't it vexing to have Monsieur Tonson come again? "

MR. DANE TO M. N., SEPTEMBER 21.

" ' God moves in a mysterious way,' etc. B. & H.'s proposition does not much surprise me, though it is an entire change of base, not to say baseness. They now propose exactly what I wanted at first, a reference to some fair man ; and had I made a list of a half-dozen for them to choose from, Mr. Rogers would probably have been one of them. He is quite deaf, but transacts business, and it is for him to say whether he is fit to *hear* the matter. Of course you are at liberty to name another or others. I have great confidence that any man of such a character will do what he thinks is just. . . . .

" Now let me say this is getting to be a serious matter ; and though you may doubtless look on it as very plain, you may be much embarrassed before you are through.

" I do not see how you can decline their offer, which is precisely your own, if you took the formality out as I suggested. I doubt now whether B. & H. will not find some way to avoid a hearing. I think you had better accept their offer, but with limitations that shall hold them somewhere. In any reference of this sort, it will be understood that you may have counsel and witnesses, unless the idea is excluded by agreement. . . . .

" You see I bear your burdens almost instinctively. In fact, I fear to trust you alone, you being, after all, but a poor little creeter, bless you."

M. N. TO MR. DANE, SEPTEMBER 23.

" Your letter did me heaps of good, yesterday.

" Mr. Robertson promises to find out the ways of
the Corinthian publishers, and write or tell me. . . . .
What I want to do, if I do anything, is to make
out a written statement, as you suggest, but appear
only by that and you.   I don't want myself to go
on the stage.   I should injure the case more than I
should help it.   Everything that is not in writing,
you know as well as I, and I think it would be far
better for me to stay at home, the sweet, safe corner
by the household fire, behind the heads of children,
la ! In every other suggestion I agree with you. . . . .
I could make my statement, send it to you for decision and presentation, notify them of my acceptance
and readiness, and then let the Union slide.

" Did I tell you I had a nice note from *Longinus?*
. . . . He says he wants to talk with me about this —
that he thinks authors ought to have an understanding, — that generally with B. & H. he has such and
such arrangements ; but he marks that whatever
arrangement you make, the publisher generally
gets the lion's share.

" Now do you think there is any hurry ?   If not
— and as they have wandered at their own sweet
will hitherto, I think I might take my turn now ;
do you think it will be worth while for me to give

up my visit? Considering the uncertainty of man, I should say not."

MR. DANE TO M. N., SEPTEMBER 24.

" There is no reason why you should hurry about your B. & H. matter. They have not been in great haste even to answer your letters. Wherefore, although I shall be glad to see you very soon, you may take your own time, and by thinking, perhaps, add a cubit to your mental stature.

" I am not quite sure you can be excused from being present. You can, however, fortify or fiftify yourself with Fritz or Fred.

" Now write down your claims against B. & H. like a lawyer."

About this time, the Athenian press seemed to have been seized with an unwonted interest in the book trade, and began to break out in sapient and significant little paragraphs like the following, which I copy from the " Athenian Tribune," of September 30, 1768:—

" BOOK PUBLISHING.—There is no class of business so liable to misconstruction and misunderstanding, as that of a publisher of books. It is difficult for an author to understand the business aspects of publishing a book. In the first place, the expenses of composition, correcting, stereotyping, paper, printing and binding, are very large, compared sometimes to the size of the book. Then the advertising bills, and two or three hundred gratuitous copies for notice and review, must be added to the cost of publication. Then, of course, store rent, clerk hire, and packing expenses, including paper, twine and boxes, should be reckoned as part of the cost of getting up an edition of a book; so that, in most instances, the sale of two or three thousand of a new work hardly pays the publisher for the labor and capital included in the outlay. Now all this the author, unless he or she happen to understand the business thoroughly, rarely comprehends. The elder John Murray, one of the most honorable and generous of publishers, used to say, that an author who thoroughly understood all the intricacies and expenses of issuing a book from the press, and properly launching it into the hands of the public, was as rare a prize to find as a phœnix or a unicorn."

Yes.

When I came to reflect upon the matter, the proposal of B. & H. did not seem so much like my own as it at first appeared. Partly, perhaps, I feared the Greeks even bearing gifts. And if the two plans were in substance the same, why did they suggest one so soon after rejecting the other? If they were not the same, the difference would not be likely to be in my favor. The superficial thinker might suggest that the person to judge whether formal arbitration would be satisfactory to me was myself. As I had proposed it, the information from Messrs. B. & II. that it would not be satis- factory to *me*, seemed to be premature, not to say supererogatory. But they not only set aside formal arbitration and brought up a " confidential friendly " plan — not with a suggestion that it might, but with the succinct assertion that it would answer the same end in a much better way; they also chose the con- fidential friend themselves ; and this friend was a gentleman with whom I had no acquaintance, whom I had never so much as seen, and of whom my personal knowledge was confined to the inter- change of some half dozen letters. Now a man may have a very high reputation, and be a very superior person, yet when you want a confidential friend, you would hardly take him, unless you had, at least, a passing acquaintance with him. Per- haps Messrs. B. & II.'s endorsement of any one as a " just man," ought to be enough ; though, under the circumstances, it reminds one of the convicts in the Maine state prison, who drew up resolutions against capital punishment, — but regarding the confidential friendly way of doing business, I had become thoroughly disenchanted. It was confidential friendliness that made the trouble, and I was not homœopathically inclined. I languished for a little distrustful business accuracy, and cried, "Save me from my friends," or rather from Messrs. B. & H.'s friends.

What philosopher was it who maintained that life and death are the same? "Why do you not then kill yourself?" asked a skeptic. "Because they are the same."

If it was of no importance to Messrs. B. & H. whether we had one man or two, I would have two, since it was of no importance.

If it was important to them that we should not have two, then I would have two, because it was important.

M. N. TO B. & H., NEAR THE LAST OF OCTOBER.

"I accept your proposal, that the matter at issue between us should be submitted to Mr. Samuel Rogers, for decision, with this modification, that Mr. James Russell, of Stanton, be associated with him. If they have any difficulty in coming to an agreement, let us empower them to select a third person.

"I will present my statement at any time that suits your and their convenience.

"Permit me, however, to suggest that it is just as much work for me to prepare my case for two or

three persons as it is for two or three thousand ; and,
after all, nobody can know it better than you.
You know precisely what I want, — simply ten per
cent. And you know also on what grounds I base
my claims. Would it not be less troublesome to
you, as well as infinitely less disagreeable to me, for
you to decide the matter yourselves at once, rather
than refer it to others, who, after the most careful
study, can only learn what we already know ? We
shall also thereby avoid a publicity which is utterly
distasteful to me, which can hardly be attractive to
you, and which, beginning with two, will end, no
one knows where."

HUNT, PARRY, & CO. (FORMERLY B. & H.) TO M. N.,
NOVEMBER 9.

" The preoccupation incident to the recent
change in our firm (of which we sent you a notice)
has prevented our giving your proposal due consideration earlier than now.

" We proposed Mr. Samuel Rogers' name, with
the thought that he was a man who would be in
every way satisfactory to both parties, and who could
act rather in the capacity of a friendly mediator
than that of a formal arbitrator.

" Our objection to the addition of Mr. James
Russell, is, that by adding him we return to the
idea of settling differences by a formal arbitrator,

which we always objected to.   We should prefer
to submit the entire matter to Mr. Rogers alone,
as we proposed.   Still we are desirous to have
the matter settled justly and equitably, and if
you prefer to have more than one person, we
are willing that Mr. Russell (of whom we know
nothing, except by reputation) should be added,
provided a third person shall be joined with the two,
who shall be a practical publisher and bookseller.
We would name a gentleman who would be perfectly capable of appreciating *all* the points connected with the case, and to whom, in conjunction
with the two already named, we are willing to submit it, — Mr. Henry Murray, formerly a partner in
the publishing firm of Constable & Sons, and now
the head of the firm of Murray & Blakeman. Mr.
Murray is a highly honorable man, and from his
many years of experience, fully qualified to understand the case.

" If you are willing to submit the case to these
three gentlemen for decision, we shall await your
and their pleasure as to time."

M. N. TO H., P., & CO., NOVEMBER 17.

" Your letter of November 9 has been for-
warded to me from Athens.   Your notice of the
change in the firm was probably sent to Zoar and
has not reached me.   I did not know of the change
when my letter was written.

" In proposing Mr. Russell I did not design to return to formal arbitration. I was, and am, quite willing to settle it by confidential friendliness, only I do not wish the friendliness to be all on one side. Mr. Rogers is your friend, but I never saw him; cannot judge of his fitness to act in such a matter, and therefore could not put implicit faith in his conclusions. I wish to associate with him a man whom I do know, and on whose conclusions I could rely.

" You say you know nothing of Mr. Russell except by reputation; neither do I know anything of Mr. Rogers except by reputation.

" You desire to join with them Mr. Murray of the firm of Murray & Blakeman, a gentleman whom you know so well that you vouch for his character and capacity, but whom I never saw, whom I scarcely know even by reputation, but of whom I do know this: Soon after the publication of ' The Rights of Men,' the firm, of which he is the head, issued an advertisement of one of their publications by Rev. Bishop Burnet, in which, by detaching sentences from ' The Rights of Men,' they made me speak in the highest praise of Bishop Burnet's book, whereas, in truth, I had spoken with the greatest censure. You say that Mr. Murray is a highly honorable man, but I say that this was a highly dishonorable proceeding.

" Observe now the position you take. *You* are

not even willing to trust to my friend, joined with
your friend, but you want me to trust to your friend
alone.

"Secondly, you are not willing to refer to the
arbitrator, a lawyer, whom you have selected, and
the arbitrator, a lawyer, whom I have selected, and
the third person whom they two shall select, but
you wish yourself to select the third person, and
the person you select is a man of your own trade, a
man of your intimate acquaintance, a man whom I
never saw, and of whom personally I only know
that he has been guilty of trickery toward me.

"If it is to be settled by confidential friendship,
you wish to choose the confidential friend. If by
formal arbitration, you wish to choose two out of
three of the arbitrators.

"You consider Mr. Rogers quite capable of settling the matter alone, but incapable of settling it in
connection with a friend of mine, unless another
friend of yours be joined with him.

"I am quite willing to meet you on the confidential friendly platform, or on the formal arbitration
platform; but if the former, which I also prefer, I
wish to have a share in the confidential friendship.
If the second, I wish the arbitrators to be selected
in the regular way, each party choosing one, and
those two selected choosing a third.

"You can ascertain from Mr. Rogers whether

he has any objection to confidential consultation
with Mr. Russell. So far as a practical publisher
or bookseller is concerned you can state the case
yourselves to these gentlemen, — or you can bring
Mr. Murray or any other person you choose before
them. We must assume that they are sufficiently
fair-minded to judge according to facts, else there
is no use in having any judgment at all, and Mr.
Murray can present the facts as witness quite as
well as if he were arbitrator."

H., P., & CO. TO M. N., NOVEMBER 20.

"The desire which you impute to us of having
a one-sided settlement, or of referring the matter
at issue between us to any "confidential friend"
of our own has never entered our thoughts. We
named Mr. Rogers in the first instance because we
thought he was a warm personal friend of your
own, and one in whom you could put unhesitating
confidence. We never had a word with him on
the subject in any way. As for Mr. Murray, we
certainly have no desire to press him, or any other
person not agreeable to you.

"We very decidedly prefer that *one* person shall
take cognizance of the matter rather than *two* or
three; and to show that we do not desire that the
person chosen shall be a partisan of our own, we
suggest that the matter be submitted to the friendly

offices of Mr. Henry Brook, of Corinth. We do not know Mr. Brook personally, and have never had any relations with him except a correspondence which he initiated several days ago. If he is willing to act in the matter we, will accept any decision he makes."

M. N. TO H., P., & CO., NOVEMBER 23.

" Your letter of November 20 reached me Saturday night. So far as it disclaims any undue partisanship in selecting Mr. Rogers, it is germane to the case. I take the earliest opportunity to thank you for the disinterested kindness to me which governed your choice. I was not before aware of it, or I should have been earlier in my acknowledgment.

" The remainder of your letter, you will pardon me for saying, is entirely irrelevant. The question of one or two is no longer open. We have already agreed upon two, and the question now is concerning a third. The point to be decided is simply this : Will you or will you not refer the matter to the friendly mediation or the formal arbitration of Messrs. Rogers and Russell and a third person to be selected by them in case a third person shall be necessary ?"

H., P., & CO. TO M. N., NOVEMBER 28.

"Your statement, that 'the question of one or two persons is no longer open, and that two have already been agreed upon, and the question now is concerning a third,' is not correct. *We* have not agreed to refer the matter to Messrs. Rogers and Russell except with our proposed addition of Mr. Murray, which addition you did not approve. By your non-approval of him the matter was thrown back to the original proposal to refer it to one person, and in that posture of affairs we must consider that our proposal of Mr. Brook as that person was strictly relevant.

"But in all this correspondence we seem to be playing at cross-purposes, neither arriving at a result nor succeeding in understanding each other. You are no doubt as tired of this as we are. A reference — should we ever reach it on mutually satisfactory terms — would take a long time and be a tedious mode of settlement. Would it not be better to close the matter at issue finally by a definite proposal which cannot be misunderstood. We estimate the time that would be occupied by a reference, and the trouble and annoyance it would occasion, at five hundred dollars, and we propose to send you our check for that sum that this unprofitable controversy may be closed. And we further pro-

pose to pay you hereafter ten per cent. of the
retail price, in cloth, for all copies sold of your various books now published by us. Should you accept
this offer, please advise us and we will send you
check and draw new contracts at once."

I think, notwithstanding the modest disclaimer
of Messrs. Hunt, Parry, & Co., we were getting to
understand each other perfectly, except that so far
from becoming tired of the controversy, *I* was only
just warming up to it.

M. N. TO H., P., & CO., DECEMBER 8.

" When I pointed out to you the impropriety of
your imposing Mr. Murray upon me as arbitrator,
you replied that you did not wish to press Mr. Murray. You now say that Mr. Murray was essential
to the arbitration. Either he was or he was not.
If he was, then, as I said in a previous letter, you
refused arbitration unless you could choose two out
of three of the arbitrators, and those two friends of
your own and strangers to me, and one of them
guilty of trickery towards me. If Mr. Murray was
not essential, then, as I said in my last letter, we
had already agreed upon two, and the only question
is, concerning a third. Do I understand you to
decide that you refuse arbitration unless you have
power to make Mr. Murray third arbitrator ?

" The reference which seems to you so tedious, seems to me a relief from tedium. Your definite proposal proposes to buy me off from arbitration, but does not touch my claim to ten per cent. on past sales. I do not even consider it, much less accept it.

" The cost of arbitration would, I suppose, be defrayed as usual by the losing party, and amounts to hardly if any more than one-sixth part of the sum which I believe to be due me."

M. N. TO H., P., & CO., DECEMBER 21.

" A week ago, last Tuesday, I sent you a letter from Paris, to which I have received no answer. To guard against any misunderstanding arising from a lost letter, will you be so good as to inform me by the bearer whether you have received such a letter from me, and if so, whether you have replied to it."

They evidently thought the enemy was preparing to move immediately upon their works, and they replied at once, —

" We duly received your communication alluded to in your note of this morning.

" Owing to the absence of one of the members of our firm and the great pressure of business incident to the season of the year, we have not had an opportunity since its receipt to give the question at issue the attention it deserves. In a very few days you shall hear from us."

On the sixteenth of December, appeared another of those paragraphs in the "Athenian Gazette," to which I have previously referred. Hitherto the dove had only gyrated around the whole heavens, spreading its white wings of praise over publishers in general, but now, loving, like Death, a shining mark, it circled down and settled squarely upon the modest brows of Messrs. Brummell & Hunt, in the following style : —

"MESSRS. B. & H.'s ANNOUNCEMENTS. — The attractive advertisement of Messrs. B. & H., which appears in our columns to-day, is interesting to those who watch the progress of events, as an indication not only of the success which this publishing house has achieved, but as an evidence of the literary supremacy of the 'hub.' Years ago, when Sophocles, after enjoying the entree into the leading social circles of the city, styled Athens 'The Modern Eden,' our neighbors of the other cities quoted the remark in derision. But time has proved that the title was not merely complimentary. A glance at the list of authors whose works are published by Messrs. B. & H., will at once surprise those unacquainted with the large number of the *Adriatic* coterie who have residence within the shadow of the Acropolis. The Athenian authors who have their established headquarters with this publishing house are more widely known and more thoroughly read than any equal number who have acquired literary distinction, while the number of Roman authors who are represented in this country by Messrs. B. & H. include the Poet Laureate of Italy and the great master of fiction, Josephus.

"While we may congratulate the firm upon the success they have achieved in producing the most exquisite illustrated gift books of the season, and compliment them upon the typographical execution of all their publications, we think still higher praise is due to this house for their encouragement of Athenian talent, and their rare tact in introducing many who have become popular mainly by the discriminating manner in which they have been ushered into the presence of the reading public. Whatever share of prosperity this publishing house has reached, there are none to attribute it to any narrow or selfish policy. They have dealt with authors of all lands upon the broad ground of mutual benefit, and have never sought to make bread out of other people's brainwork and leave the worker without fair compensation. It is a credit to Athens that such an establishment has grown up and flourished in our city."

Which reminds me of a rural schoolmaster who taught the village school for several winters in succession, and whose specialty was writing. Years after, if the handwriting of any of his pupils was spoken of, the honest man would reply innocently, " Yes, he is a very fine writer, very superior. His writing is precisely like mine ! "

Messrs. Brummel & Hunt's authors are the most widely known and the most thoroughly read in the country.

And we who belong to that Happy Family feel that the lines have fallen to us in pleasant places, and try to look unconscious of our preëminence, while we cannot wholly repress a glow of gratification.

But what is this ? We, or rather you, — for just here I find it agreeable to follow the admonition of Mr. Guppy's mother, and " get out " of the company — *you* have become popular mainly by the discriminating manner in which you have been ushered into the presence of the reading public ! O, what a fall is here, my countrymen ! Imagine the emotions of the belle on being told that the attention and admiration which she fondly supposed had been excited by her wit and beauty, were mainly owing to the discriminating manner in which she had been ushered into the ball-room !

Some little margin is left for grace of form, loveliness of feature, elegance of dress, but mainly it is the white-gloved usher to whom her success is due !

There are never wanting persons who, not content with writing history as it is, are always conjuring up what would have been if things had happened differently. If Charles I. had not lost his head, if Napoleon had beaten at Waterloo, if Booth's pistol had missed fire, events would have gone thus and thus. A fruitful field opens before such speculators in the history of our country's literature. Had Messrs. Brummell & Hunt gone into the grocery business, for instance, Homer would have been cobbling shoes in Haverhill, or at most, chronicling small beer in a country newspaper. Dante would have been a lawyer in chambers, drawing up wills and plodding through deeds, but leaving no foot-prints on the sands of time. Boccaccio would have been milking cows at Brook Farm, or growing round shouldered over his desk in the Jerusalem Court House. Miriam would have been writing children's stories for the " Little Cormorant," at fifty cents a column, and as Uncle Tom's Cabin would never have been built, the South would never have been provoked into rebellion; we should have had no war and no greenbacks, prices would never have risen, ten per cent. and fifteen cents would have been the same, and we should all have died comfortably in our beds.

But it is a theme for lasting gratitude not only that this house did not go into the "cotton trade and sugar line," but also that whatever share of prosperity it has reached, there are none to attribute it to any narrow or selfish policy. It has never sought to make bread out of other people's brain-work and leave the worker without fair compensation. But upon what meat hath this our "Athens Gazette" fed, that it is able to make so sweeping a negative, asks the unsanctified heart. By what authority saith it these things, and who gave it this authority? Has it had personal interviews with all the persons who ever had or sought business connections with Messrs. Brummel & Hunt, and learned from them that no narrow or selfish policy has ever been attributed to them? Even this would not establish its assertion, but surely nothing less than this would. It does not say that no narrow or selfish policy was ever indulged in, but that nobody so much as attributed it to them. Cæsar's wife is above suspicion. But has any one asked Cæsar?

It is not, of course, to be for a moment supposed that so great a house as the one in question would ever stoop to manufacture its own "puffs," if I may be pardoned the term. Such a course might befit the "parvenu hawkers and peddlers" of books, but not an hereditary aristocracy like this. Its "Poet-Publisher" has indeed distinguished himself by other figures than those of the day-book and ledger,

but I have never heard that any member of the firm
has been ambitious of a place among the prose writers of Greece. Nor is it I suspect any the more
to be presumed because these paragraphs came to
me conspicuously marked with blue and red lines,
and superscribed in the handwriting with which
many years of correspondence with the firm of B. &
H. had made me familiar. For do we not all, as
soon as we see ourselves complimented in the
newspaper, send it around to all our friends by
the early mail? But I am reminded of a story
which I learned and recited many times in school.
While the regicides Goffe, Whalley, and Maxwell
were hiding in Connecticut, a rough fellow came
from afar and terrified the simple villagers by chal-
lenging them to mortal combat. As they stood
pale with consternation, a venerable man, unknown
to all, appeared, gravely accepted the challenge, and
immediately disappeared. At the appointed time
throngs were gathered to witness the conflict. As
the clock struck the hour, the mysterious combat-
ant threaded the crowd and took his place in the
arena armed only with a broom, and armored with
a huge cheese fastened upon his person as a breast-
plate. The astonished bully began the fight by
plunging his sword into the breast, or rather the
cheese, of his opponent. The latter responded by
dipping his broom into the neighboring mud-puddle

and giving the bully a gentle swash about the neck.
A second lunge into the cheese, and the broom
went higher, sweeping the fighter's chin.   A third,
and with a fresh baptism of mud the broom was
drawn tenderly over the whole face of the baffled
ruffian, who, unused to such warfare, threw down
his sword in terror, crying, " Who are you ?   You
must be either Goffe, Whalley, or the Devil ! "

Moral: So I, viewing this paragraph and sundry
others that follow it, and seeing how finely they are
timed to the issues of the contest, cannot avoid
the mental soliloquy, " Brummell & Hunt, or —
Planchette ! "

J. S. PARRY, OF THE FIRM OF H., P., & CO., TO M. N., JANUARY 1, 1769.

" The experience of the past few months suggests
that it is likely to take some time to settle the details
of the proposed arbitration by correspondence.   A
personal interview of half an hour would obviate
much writing and delay.   Will you see me at
Zoar at such time next week (after Tuesday) as
may be convenient to yourself?

M. N. TO MR. PARRY.

" If you really think it worth while, by all means
come ; only the preliminaries seem to me so simple

that they might almost be left to whistle themselves. I will see you, if you please, at two o'clock,
P. M., Wednesday, the sixth, — day after to-morrow.
A train leaves the Athens Railroad Station, I think,
at 12.15. You must leave the train at Zoar. Probably there will be a carriage at the station if you
prefer it to walking, but whichever way you come
you will wish you had taken the other.

M. N. TO MR. DANE, JANUARY 4, 1769.

" Saturday I had a letter from Mr. Parry, proposing to come down and arrange with me the preliminaries for (or of) arbitration. I would much
rather he should go to you and do it. Still, I fear
if I suggest that, it will only occasion further delay,
and if I can get any hold on them, perhaps I had
better get it. But I don't know what the preliminaries ought to be. Maybe it is nothing in particular, only arrangements as to time, and so forth.
Still, if there is anything I should stipulate for, or
any boundary lines I ought to draw, or any precau-
tions I ought to take, can you not advise me by letter? If there is any doubt on my part, I shall make
no engagements, but say to him frankly, I wish to
consult you first, and then I shall come to Athens
bright and early, Thursday, and *consult* you *nolens
volens.*"

MR. DANE TO M. N., JANUARY 5, 1769.

" A happy New Year to you.   My opinion is that
Mr. Parry will try to *settle* matters with you, and
have no reference or intervention.   If he proposes
to arrange a reference, you know what you want
and can write it, perhaps, though my honest opinion
is you need help.   You may call it snubbing, or sneer-
ing, or flattery, but my opinion is you are not fit to
meet these people in such a matter.

" Hunt fooled you just as he pleased when he
went over, and you wrote me quite a penitent letter, which showed a good heart, but a feeble mind !
If you arrange for any reference, they should agree
to pay you any amount that may be adjudged to be
equitably due to you for arrearages of copyright.

" You are [&c.]   But as I have told you, there
is not a lawyer in Athens who would undertake
personally to manage a controversy of this kind,
being himself the party, and you are not exempt
from the laws of gravitation." . . . .

VIII.

ARRANGEMENT OF PRELIMINARIES.

T the appointed time, Mr. Parry presented himself. But instead of proceeding, at once, to settling the preliminaries of the proposed arbitration, he wished to discuss the question at issue to see if we could not settle it between ourselves. I unhesitatingly declined, as I had from the beginning declined to do so. He said he had brought with him the papers and figures to show exactly how we stood. I declined to look at them, telling him that I was entirely incompetent to make a satisfactory examination of such a point, being unsound even on the multiplication-table. He asked if I would not be satisfied, supposing they could clearly prove that I had made more money out of the books than they had. I said not at all, that I had arrived at that point where I did not, in the least, care how much the publishers made; that if other authors had ten per cent., I wanted ten per cent., even if the publishers had to beg their bread from door to door. He seemed a little nonplused at such heartlessness; said he had come prepared to

show that they had made only about seven tenths
as much as I, and he had supposed that would satisfy me.   As I affirmed it would not, he was somewhat at a loss how to proceed.   I told him that in
the beginning, that — and a great deal less, indeed
— would have satisfied me, but that affairs had
gone on so long, and feeling been so much aroused,
that no sort of explanation would satisfy me ; that I
wished the matter to go entirely away from ourselves into the hands of unprejudiced and uninter-
ested persons.

[After several months of profound reflection, I
will here interpolate a remark which future com-
mentators will please to remember does not belong
to the original text, namely : that I do not see why
the publisher's profits need be considered as the *ulti-
ma Thule* of an author's.   Is it the phantom of a dis-
torted imagination that the author has a far larger
property in the book than the publisher?   Does
it not cost him infinitely more than it costs the publisher ?   And even leaving the infinite, and coming
down to finite matters, are not the fields which the
publisher reaps so much broader than the author's
one little close, that a far smaller share in the
gleanings would give the publisher a far more heap-
ing granary.   An author, we will say, publishes
one book in a year.   His profits are a thousand
dollars.   But the publisher publishes twenty books

a year, on which, in the same ratio, he gets twenty
thousand dollars. Suppose five hundred dollars
were taken from the publisher's profits and added
to the author's. The publisher would still have an
income of ten thousand dollars, while the author
would have one of only fifteen hundred.]

Mr. Parry then suggested leaving it to Mr. Stan-
hope, one of my friends, a suggestion which I did
not adopt. He asked me if I still continued to
prefer that it should be left to more than one person, and I left him no doubt on that point. He
then suggested that we should give up the two
we had chosen, and select entirely new ones. I
assured him that I was not in the least dissatisfied
with their choice or my own, and I would prefer to
make no change. He suggested that Mr. Rogers
was very hard of hearing, and might not be able to
act on that account. I asked if he was materially
harder of hearing now than when they selected him
to settle the case alone. Mr. Parry did not know
that he was, and finally consented to go on as we
had begun. This, in the telling, does not sound
quite straightforward, yet Mr. Parry seemed so
frank and fair that I was more than half convinced,
in spite of all other appearances, that they meant
no wrong. At least I did not see how any one
could be conscious of wrong, and yet seem so honest
as he seemed. He was certainly entirely courteous,

though, perhaps, it is not parliamentary to put that in. One tenth part of his fairness in the beginning would have set my doubts completely at rest. He said — but tenderly enough, as if he loved me à la Isaak Walton — that they lost money on " Holidays," and that the books have not been selling very well for two years past. For all which I am very sorry. Still I remember that Mr. Hunt was always urgent for me to make books. The last two books were published in book form at his suggestion. My first notion was to publish them as magazine articles. The same was the case with "Old Miasmas." They grew into books, and I have just found an old letter in which Mr. Hunt says, " Come out with a bang. The book's the thing in which you will catch the conscience of the public." And again, " A volume by all means." Nothing could be more encouraging, and stimulating, and agreeable than his tone and bearing. I recollect his saying to me, when we were discussing the last book, " You ought to write only books." In a letter of October 23, 1767, he says, " I think you are quite right not to print your Burnet article at present, and I hope your thoughts will grow into a volume to be issued by B. & H., in the spring." In a letter of December 11, 1765, he says, " Your sermon is good, but I hope you will not print it till you put it into a volume. Ask Brother S., your neigh-

bor, if I am not right. If you were here, I could
tell you a thousand reasons *why* your interest would
not be served in the printing of this paper in a newspaper or magazine, nor the interest of the reading
world, either. I speak as a fool, no doubt, but in
your service.

"I hope you will give all your energy and time to
'Winter Work.' A new book from your pen in the
spring will help the old ones, and is already asked
for by our booksellers in the West and elsewhere."

In short, as I look back, it seems to me that Mr.
Hunt's influence — always pleasantly and heartily
exerted — was towards the production and not the
repression of books. I deeply regret that they have
not enriched him to the extent of his desires and
deserts, and I should regret it still more deeply had
I urged the publications upon him as warmly as he
urged them upon me.

Although the firm lost money on "Holidays,"
this paper shows that they were ready to accept
another juvenile book as soon as I told them of its
existence. I suppose there is some occult reason
for it, known only to publishers; but the carnal
mind would naturally infer that having lost money
on one, they would be shy of a second venture.

Mr. Parry repeated Mr. Hunt's assertion, that
he replied with his own hand to my first letter of
inquiry. Mr. Hunt, in speaking of it to me, could

9

not recall the exact time of his writing it, but Mr. Parry said that Mr. Hunt told him that morning, that it was written directly after the reception of my letter. But in a letter written two or three weeks after mine was sent, Mr. Hunt says by his amanuensis, "I have *not* answered your last letter touching the terms expressed in the contracts." Mr. Hunt apparently labors under the curious psychological infelicity of remembering the letters he does not write, and forgetting the letters he does write.

After Mr. Parry had told me that my books had not been selling well for a year or two, and that they had lost money on them, I hunted up old letters of Mr. Hunt's to see if they would not show that he had urged me to write in the form of books. In doing so I found a letter dated September 23, 1764, from which I make the following extract: "The contract has been delayed for a sufficient cause." (He then gives as a reason Mr. Brummell's absence.) "The percentage will read fifteen cents per copy, as the business times are fluctuating the prices of manufacture so there is no telling to-morrow or for a new edition what may be the expenses of publication, so we reckon your percentage in every and any event as fixed at fifteen cents per volume on all your works. If it should cost $1.50 to make the volumes you are sure of your author profit of fifteen cents. The price at retail may be $1.50, $2.00, or $3.00, as the high or low rates of paper, binding, etc., may be, but *you* are all right. This arrangement we make now with all our authors."

If I had discovered this letter sooner it would have simplified matters greatly; but I did not find it till this statement had been, as I supposed, finished. I therefore thought best to put it in here, in a sort of chronological order. What I had previously said touching its substance, I said from memory solely. I could not even have declared whether its assertions had been made by pen or lips. But I think it not only fully bears out all that I have alleged, but shows more than my memory had retained or my perception divined. The letter before its close says, "As I write the contracts are reported ready, so I enclose them. Sign both and send back the one marked with red ✕. You keep one and we the other."

I see now that in case the books *had* gone up to $3.00, I should have been sure of my author profits of fifteen cents and "all right," even if I had continued on the old terms of ten per cent; but I did not see it then, nor anything else, for that matter. The reasoning of this process is not a little remarkable. Prices of all kinds are changing, therefore your price shall not change. And what kind of percentage is that which is no percentage at all but an unchangeable quantity ?

I made direct inquiries of all the authors accessible to me, whose works were in the hands of Messrs. Brummell & Hunt, at or about that time. I received information from some fifteen different persons. With no one of them did Messrs. Brummell & Hunt make the arrangement they made with me. Nine reported receiving ten per cent. Some received half profits. One received twelve cents on a book that retailed at a dollar and a quarter. One said that he received twelve cents on a dollar and a half book and ten cents on a dollar and a quarter. Another that he receives ten per cent. sometimes but not always.

Mr. Hunt often urged upon me the advantage and importance of my writing only for them ; so that, with the exception of the " Segregationalissuemost," for which I was writing when I began with Messrs. Brummell & Hunt, I have neither in periodical or book, written for any other house than theirs. It might seem as if this injunction of his, all friendly and judicious as it may have been, did put them under something like an obligation to do as well by me as any other house would do.

When " City Lights " was published, its retail price was a dollar and a quarter, and the first account allows me twelve and a quarter cents a volume. Mr. Parry said that the retail price of the books was changed five or six times after my percentage was changed to a fixed sum. The latter change was made in the autumn of 1764. In a copy of "Rocks of Offense," date 1764, the advertised retail price of all the books is one dollar and a half. "Old Miasmas" was published in the autumn of 1764, and was, from the beginning, sold at two dollars. These are the only prices that I have seen or heard of since the first. Mr. Parry, however, says they have at two different times been held at one dollar and seventy-five cents. I think those times must have been of very short duration, as I never saw those prices advertised, and never knew of their existence. I have inquired incognito of the principal booksellers in Athens and not one of them was aware that the price had ever been put down since it was put up. But, with all the changes, the difficulties of computing percentage can hardly have been insurmountable.

Mr. Parry at this time told me what I did not know before,— that the publishers reserved to themselves in the first contract for " City Lights " fifteen hundred books. The contract specifies only the first edition. I suppose an edition has no prescribed size ; but I have never in any other case known more than the first thousand being reserved to the publishers.

" City Lights " was published September, 1762. On the first of December of the same year Mr. Hunt reported that before January it would have gone to a fourth edition. I should like to know if each of those four editions numbered fifteen hundred volumes. What, for instance, was the size of the second edition, or the third ?

After careful inquiry I found no one in the "regular line " paying or receiving less than ten per cent., with the possible exceptions I have mentioned. Mr. Dickson was assured by a prominent member of the firm, that the Troubadours never think in any case of offering less than ten per cent. on the retail price, and that in some cases they pay twelve and a half or fifteen. He is confident that there has been no change within the last few years, and that ten per cent. is the current copyright with all reputable publishers, not only in Corinth, but in other cities. He says an instance occurred with one of their writers in which they agreed to pay a certain amount per volume ; but as there was an implied understanding that it was so much per cent. on the retail price, the matter was compromised between publishers and author when prices went up."

M. N. TO MR. DANE, JANUARY 7, 1769.

"Your letter made me laugh, and so did me good, like a medicine. By turning to the latter

pages of my bulky book you will find the gist of
Mr. P.'s errand here. He desired first to explain
the matters to me, then to refer to Mr. S., then
to take two new men, but I persuaded him out of
them all. . . . . He was to communicate with Mr.
Russell to-day, and I expect to hear the result to-
morrow. I am in hopes to have the thing begun
on Saturday, if we can make forty ends meet. Mr.
Parry thinks it will take several days, as he says
they shall bring out their books for examination; —
shall not confine themselves to the prescribed custom of publishers to pay ten per cent. but shall
bring in other things, I don't know what, — their figures, I suppose, to show what an unprofitable thing
publishing is. He was uncertain whether Mr. Rogers would consent to act. I begged Mr. P. to say to
him that I should not consider it any hostility to me.
· Mr. P. suggested that I write it to him and I did.
Can you appear on Saturday, in case they agree
to meet? I don't want to come out myself. I send
you here a little book for you to look upon like
John Rogers, and I think that will answer far better than I could. I will send you also my accounts
in case you might want them. I believe you have
the contracts. You can read the statement I suppose, or simply present it and let them read it themselves. . . . .

"I would have preferred that you should see Mr.

Parry, but I could find no sufficient excuse for not
seeing him myself, and I feared it might be offensive to insist upon your presence. . . . . But as it
was, Mr. Parry apparently had no mischievous intent. He said they should pay if the arbitrators so
decided, but seemed particularly desirous that I also
should agree to accept the decision and fully to ex-
onerate B. & H. in case the decision should be for
them, and that I should say so to my friends and
those who had been made acquainted with my dissatisfaction. Of course it would be infamous not to
do that. I was very favorably impressed. It seems
as if they must be honest or he could not appear as
he did, but I assure you I did not 'gush' in the
least. I told him I should accept the decision as
far as regarded the past before this year, but all
the world could not convince me that they had met
me fairly and satisfactorily since I began to investigate ; that I thought their course had been such as
to aggravate and even to originate suspicion.'

HUNT, PARRY, & CO. TO M. N., JANUARY 7, 1769.

" We have had an interview with Mr. Russell
this morning. He agrees with us that it would not
be wise to enter into the business of the reference
without ample time to consider all the points involved, especially as Mr. Rogers declines positively
to act, and we are now compelled to choose another

referee. Mr. Russell is obliged to leave for London on Saturday night ; and he on the whole prefers to come to Athens some four weeks hence if need be, or on his return from the Witenagemote the 1st of March. We trust this will be satisfactory to you.

" For the associate of Mr. Russell in the case, we select the Hon. G. W. Hampden, late member of Witenagemote from this city. The two gentlemen are well known to each other. Please inform us if he is satisfactory to you ; and also please inform us if it is your wish that a third person should be chosen by these two before a hearing be had, or only in the event of their disagreeing."

M. N. TO MR. DANE.

" So here it is you see, apparently as far off as ever. What do you say? I think I have heard that Mr. Hampden is a large paper-manufacturer, and also that the House have their paper of him. If so I think it would not be best that he should be the one, but I don't wish to be *cantankerous.* I will not answer them till I hear from you."

MR. DANE TO M. N., JANUARY 9.

" When you have practiced law thirty years, man and boy, as I have, you will know that any business that requires the presence of five or six business men at a given time and place, is of indefinite duration, and if those men are five hundred miles apart, the indefiniteness becomes definitely long, at least. You know there is to be an organization of the new Witenagemote after March 4, so that if we wait for Mr. Russell, we can have no hearing this winter. I know of no objection to Mr. Hampden."

M. N. TO H., P., & CO.

"I cannot say that it is 'satisfactory,' because nothing can be really satisfactory to me but an immediate and pacific settlement of my claims.

" To Mr. Hampden I have no personal objection whatever, but I seem to recollect, when we were all living in Paradise, before the fall, having heard Mr. Hampden spoken of by Mr. Hunt as a paper-manufacturer, with whom you had large dealings. If so would it not be almost too much to expect of human nature that it should be strictly impartial under such circumstances? I simply make the suggestion, not even being sure that it is ' founded on fact.'

" The choosing of a third person I should leave entirely with the two chosen. If they think a third unnecessary so much the better. I should certainly think two fair-minded, unprejudiced persons might get at the truth without recourse to a third."

" Our business relations with the firm of which Hon. G. W. Hampden is the head, have been for the last three or four years of the most insignificant amount, certainly not of a nature to warp his judgment in our favor. Besides Mr. Hampden is, like Mr. Russell, too honorable a man [still harping on my honor] to accept the position of a judge where his prejudices are enlisted.

" We do not understand from your letter that you object to Mr. Hampden. On hearing from you we will write to Mr. Russell, and say that the Reference only waits his convenience."

" I am advised — and the advice is in accordance with my own opinion — that I have no right to object to your choice, unless the person chosen be so undesirable that I decline arbitration rather than accept him as arbitrator. This certainly is not true in the case of Mr. Hampden. I have given you my only reason for objecting to him. Since you assure me this reason does not exist, I withdraw my objection."

" We have written to Mr. Russell to say that Mr. Hampden will meet him in London during the

week of Inauguration, and that the two gentlemen
can then fix such time for hearing the case as may
suit their own convenience."

M. N. TO MR. DANE, FEBRUARY 11.

"I believe that you have gone on a mission to
the king of the Cannibal Islands. Otherwise, as
Cicero says, where in the world are you? Nothing
is more evident than that you have given the world
a quitclaim deed of me.

"And that is why I am writing. About a fortnight ago, Mr. Woodlee, the Grand Vizier, wrote
to me saying that he should be off duty on the
4th of March, and if I liked would be very
happy, as a friend, to present my grievances to the
referees. Mr. Woodlee is an intimate friend of
mine, and when he was down to see me last summer I reno-varied my dolores at his own request.
I wrote to Mr. Woodlee at once that we must not
swap horses in crossing a stream, even though the
horse was a poor one. I did not use those words,
but that was the substance of doctrine — the poor
horse, my love, meaning you! He did not know
your connection with it, or did not remember.
Since then your intense and aggravated silence has
led me to think that perhaps you are so utterly
weary with the whole thing, and me into the bargain,
that you would hail with delight any opportunity to

bid farewell, a long farewell, to all my greatness.
If you do, here is your chance. If you write to
me and say that you should be happy to wash your
hands of me with Castile soap and three waters, I
shall weep salt tears from the briny deep, and send
on to London by next mail.

"You have had a rich time of it with me I know,
if I only meant to pay you. Well, truly, I do mean
to pay you — a little, not much — say seventy-five
cents or a dollar, — not half as much as you deserve. But I tell you now so you need not think
I am leaving your family penniless. And what I
do not pay in money, I shall make up to you in appreciation, for I think you have managed the case
with clear insight and much skill, — that is, under
my supervision. I have held you back from what
was rash and inaccurate, and between us we have
got matters pretty well in hand. Now it seems to
me that if you have held out so long it will be better for you to hold out to the end. The making-up
is about made up. To be sure I am going to re-
write my statement and shall probably continue the
process so long as it remains in my possession, but
the main points will be the same, so you will apparently have little more trouble with it. Now please
to tell me just how you feel about it — or rather, for
that is too much to ask, — just how you propose to
feel. I think you have had my 'Statement' about

long enough for your share, so I will take my turn
at holding the baby. You may send it down by express if you please, together with the bills and contracts thereunto appertaining, and let me see if it
has improved with age."

" Ungrateful Female, After all my trials and tribulations, and fault-findings at your course, you now
purpose to swap me off. Well, I will free my mind,
if I die for it. My opinion is, that neither Mr.
Woodlee, nor principalities, nor powers, nor any
other creature, can do so much for you in your trial
as I can. I believe Mr. Woodlee is a few years
younger than I and so has a greater chance to live
to the end of it *cæteris paribus*, but *cæteris* are *not
paribus*, because he lives away from the scene, and
there never could be a conjunction of Hampden,
Woodlee, Russell, etc. If I were to fly up and say
I would have nothing more to do with your case,
because you won't follow my advice, there would be
reason in it, but for you to take a new adviser —
Why you don't know how much Mr. Woodlee must
go through to be as familiar with the matter as I
am, and don't you see that you must not tax these
far-off friends in this way? I, who am your real
friend, you may do anything with, but Mr. Woodlee
and Mr. Russell never will leave all and follow you
to Athens and spend days on this trial. . . . .

"Do not be foolish unless it is really necessary. I want to make H., P., & Co. do right, and I want to do all for you that is possible. As the matter must be heard at Athens, I am the person to do it with least trouble. Your letter found me at Marathon yesterday. I shall be home next week, and your papers shall be sent. In the mean time the Lord restore you to reason. Swap me off indeed! Your *only* friend!"

M. N. TO MR. DANE, MARCH 8.

"I am bright but not quick. In short I am slow. When you inf — ex — ci — well — asked me in Oxford what I was writing my Statement for, I suppose you saw what I only just now see, — that a large part of it was not necessary. I had in mind the justification of my mode as well as of my claim, and for that the whole case needed to be unfolded. But since that letter was found, my mind has somehow clarified — the brown sugar has all turned white, and if you want to eat me while I am sweet now is your time.

"Now then, as you are a man and inexperienced, let me briefly jot down for you an outline of my proper mode of defense.

"The brief is a perfect Troy in a nutshell and all you need to plume your wings with. Read that in the Valley of Decision and immediately walk across the room to the corner where H. & P. will be cowering, and shake your fists in their face. They will reply that they do not make one author the criterion for another, whereat you will take a flying leap over all the intervening pages to the letter which says, ' This arrangement we now make with all our authors.'

" They will then bring forward their books to show that they cannot pay me more without starving themselves. You will immediately rule that out of court as not germane to the case, and the arbitrators will at once award me three thousand dollars due, and three thousand more damages, which you will bring me in gold to Zoar, and I will buy two pounds of New York candy and give a party in honor of the event. I don't see why the rest of the Statement need to be brought in at all unless, first,

" They deny that they have not made the same arrangements with all their authors. If they do, you must turn to my declaration and proof; or, second,

" They say that my mode of making my claim was so offensive that they could not notice it. This I have heard of in substance privately. If they do this then I insist upon the whole Statement's being laid before them."

M. N. TO MR. DANE, MARCH 10.

"'The sense of the dear!' as Peggotty said when Davy gave in his adhesion to her marriage on the ground of her being able to come and see him without cost of coach-hire.

"Appropos to what? Why, to your letter, of course, and a two months' session, and Dark Care sitting behind the horseman, in general.

"Isn't the tenth of March the Prince of Wales' wedding-day?

"The advantage of Halliday being in the Cabinet is, that I shall control you, you will control him, he will control Grant, and for once we shall be sure of having the government well administered.

"For my private fortunes, if I have the Lord High Chancellor for my judge, the co-Secretary of State for my fighting corps, and the Grand Vizier Suzerain for my reserve force, I shall at least fall into as well as in good company.

"Dr. Edwards used to say that if Mr. Springfield were not a sharp New England lawyer, he would be the first statesman of the day. *Mutato nomine de te fabula et pluribus unum et cetera.*

"It seems impossible to get the kink of the law out of your brain. I can stand it very well because I have you only in spots, but poor F., who has the whole vast sandy plain destitute of vegetation on her hands, must have a life of it.

10

" Behold a few of the holes which I am about to punch in your case to let in light : —

" ' We claim ten per cent.' Right.

" ' H. says it is more than you were worth, and besides you agreed to less.' Very well put and very probable.

" ' We reply, Ten per cent. is the least anybody is worth.' No we don't. We decline to enter into the question of worth, and demand the pound of flesh. They say, ' Very well, here is the bond;' and *then* we say, — ' You deceived us into our assent by,' etc., etc.

" As for their ' cruelty ' — not a bit of it. It is legitimate warfare. They made my fame by advertising, they say. Very well. I reply, first, they didn't, and second, what if they did ? If they made my sales by advertising, why did they not make A.'s in the same way ? He has never yet received a penny for the B treatise. Why not C.'s books, of which he says all that have been sold a cat could carry, and so on. On the other hand, that they have done a great deal towards circulating them I readily admit. What do I pay them ninety per cent. for, I should like to know, if not that ? Publishing is their business. That they have done more than another publisher would, I deny. They have simply transacted their business in the way they deemed most profitable to themselves. I deny that they have done anything for me out of the usual course of trade.

"About the advertising, I am indeed not fully persuaded. . . . . Possibly the books have had their day and would have fallen off any way. A fortnight or so ago, perhaps more, Mr. Smith applied to me to write for his paper. I named my price. He rather *recalcitrated*. I wrote a letter that *tickled* him, and he then proposed to come down and see me and make an arrangement. He was to be in Athens, ' the guest of his friend Mr. ———!' But in Athens he heard from "two different sources that I was less popular than I had been," and so he beat a retreat to Corinth without seeing me at all. Isn't there a wheel within a wheel?

"Is this wearing away my soul? Then my soul must be like the liver of Tityus, forever spent, renewed forever.

"If you think I don't value money, send me down a hundred dollar note and see!

"The *manner* of my making my claim is not material to the issue. No. But there is no use in wasting the time and temper of the men by unnecessary words.

"Now I beg you to disabuse your mind of the supposition that we are a court! The especial advantage of this way of settlement is, that we are not a court. . . . . You will probably little relish this letter, but it is for your good."

" I do not know whether your letter requires an answer, but as the old philosopher said, ' I have often been sorry I kept still but never was sorry I spoke.' So I will give you the benefit of the doubt.

" Ellingwood & Sampson are respectable. So far so good. I suppose they stand first in New England, don't they, by all odds ? But they are in New England, and I have conceived a distaste for New England publishing. Also they don't publish solid books such as mine, but Whately, Bacon, Wheaton, and similar light literature. Would they be as likely to do well by me as a big New York Mandarin, like the Troubadours or Pearvilles ? Do they know that my popularity is like that retired clergyman whose sands of life are nearly run out ? They will take a new book, but shall I let the old go to waste, and ought not the new to go with the old to communicate an impulse thereunto ? And is it not better to let the whole be till after arbitration, or the overthrow of the existing order of things ? I should like H., P., & Co. to be as little exasperated as possible before Gog and Magog come to close quarters. . . . . *Homer* had to pay an immense sum for one of his books which was quite out of print and of no use to the publisher. . . . . If Mr. Campton testifies that the cost of making my books is so much and the profit so much, they must admit or deny it. If they admit his figures they admit the profits which they have heretofore denied. If they deny his figures they deny profits; and how can they ask high prices for unprofitable property? If Mertons have personal grievances to redress they would be more likely to take me up *con amore*, and so I make friends of the mammon of unrighteousness. But I shall be a troublesome person hereafter to transact business with. Having once wasted my sweetness on the desert air, I shall be henceforth only the mother of vinegar. Whenever I see a publisher coming in at the front gate, I shall drop the cake-basket into the wash-boiler, slip the spoons into my pocket and keep my hand on my watch all the time I am talking with him, which might not look conciliatory. Be sure and tell Mr. Campton this, and also that there is no sale for the books, that is, if you ever say more to him about it. I don't wish to sail into anybody's good graces under false colors, and am willing to take for granted Butler's (Samuel) declaration that the pleasure is as great in being cheated as to cheat. I am not sure I shall not write a book and call it

'HARI-KARI,

OR

A CURIOSITY OF LITERATURE,'

and put The Whole Deviltry of Man into it. . . .
Is not he who compounds with wickedness as bad
as he who commits it? And oughtn't I to hold
up my beacon as a warning to all future genera-
tions? If I am not only to be fought above
ground, but am also to be undermined, shall not I
countermine?

> "' And shall Trelawney die, and shall Trelawney die,
>   Then thirty thousand Cornish boys will know the reason why!'

"I am that thirty thousand Cornish boys.

"You are not expected to answer my questions.
You can ponder them as a theme for meditation in
the night-watches."

MR. DANE TO M. N., MARCH 22.

"Mr. Hunt proposes to pass *the season* abroad
— probably will go about the time the Lord High
Chancellor & Co. are ready to hear us."

HUNT, PARRY, & CO. TO M. N., APRIL 12.

"We are in hopes of getting a meeting of our
referees early next week. Mr. Russell has advised
us of his intention of being in Athens some time
next week, and we have requested him to appoint
as early a day as possible in order to accommodate
Mr. Hampden. We trust you will be prepared to
meet the referees on any day they may appoint."

" I have been ready to meet the referees for five months, and I trust nothing will hinder me from meeting them on any day they may appoint."

A conjunction of the heavenly bodies was at length agreed upon for April 22, 1769. I mention the year for the benefit of future ages.

" To any right understanding of the questions involved in the proposed reference, it seems necessary that the referees should have information such as is indicated in the interrogatories herewith inclosed, which can come only from yourselves. If you can send me the answers before the referees meet, it may prevent delay."

The interrogatories were as follows : —

" 1. How many copies of each of the works of M. N. have been printed by your authority; how many editions of each, at what dates, and how many in each edition ?

" 2. How many copies of each of said works have you accounted to her for, and at what rate of compensation for each respectively? Please exhibit a full and exact account.

" 3. How many copies of each of the works of

the authors named below have you accounted for to said authors respectively, and at what rate per centum on the retail price of each, when reckoned by percentage, and at what price in gross when paid in gross, and upon what contract, if any, with each, for each of their works, that is to say, — A., B., C., D., E., F., G., H., I., J., K., L., M., N. ?

" 4. Had you with either of the authors named above, on the day of the date of your last contract with M. N., or to wit, on September 4th, 1764, or afterwards, and when any, and if any what agreement with either, and which of them, that such authors should receive any and what sum in gross instead of a percentage, and was such agreement written or verbal ?

" 5. What were the net profits of the ' Adriatic ' each year, from 1762 to 1767, inclusive ?

" 6. What were the net profits of the firm of Brummell & Hunt each year, from 1762 to 1767, inclusive ? "

H., P., & CO. TO MR. DANE, APRIL 19.

" We are in receipt of your note addressed to Brummell & Hunt of the 16th inst., with its inclosure.

" It seems to us premature to now consider the evidence to be used before the referees, as the ordinary preliminaries to the reference itself have not been completed."

MR. DANE TO M. N., APRIL 19.

"Your package came an hour ago, and while I was reading it came this note from H., P., & Co. It means delay, I suppose, or perchance it means if M. N. has a lawyer we will have one and put all in legal shape."

H., P., & CO. TO M. N., APRIL 21.

"On the 16th we received a communication from Mr. Nathan Dane, which led us to suppose he was acting as your attorney, and had charge of the matter of reference on your behalf. We replied to his communication, and we have heard nothing from him since."

I did not see that there was any point to any of these letters and I did not reply to them or give myself any trouble about them. If Messrs. Hunt, Parry, & Co., wanted further delay why had they agreed upon a day, and what should they want of further delay? As they had frequently had communication with Mr. Dane concerning this matter, and had themselves spoken of him as my attorney without contradiction from me, I did not quite see how they could have waited for the interrogatories, to be led to any new supposition in that respect. As to their having a lawyer, while I did not see why they should want one, I certainly had no ob-

jection. I thought Mr. Parry had come down to
Zoar on purpose to arrange the preliminaries of the
reference, and that they were sufficiently arranged
at that time. But I apprehended no trouble on
that score, and took no thought about it.

IX.

BATTLE OF GOG AND MAGOG.

WE have now reached a point in the tragedy where the English language breaks down and Pius Æneas must come to the rescue and tell —

> " Trojanas ut opes, et lamentabile regnum
> Emeruit Danai; quæque ipse miserrima vidi,
> Et quorum pars magna fui. Quis talia fando,
> Myrmidonum, Dolopumve, aut duri miles Ulyssei,
> Temperet à lachrymis?
> Sed si tantus amor (?) casus cognoscere nostros,
> Et breviter Trojæ supremum audire laborem;
> Quanquam animus meminisse horret, luctuque refugit,
> Incipiam."

And, giving the " Æneid " with some variations, I might go on —

> " Est in conspectu M. N. notissima famâ
> Insula, dives opum, agrorum et osboni dum regna manebant."

I consented to be *in conspectu* on Mr. Dane's earnest representations that matters might come up on which I was better informed than he, and on which my statements might be important.

Of course, after all this trouble, it was not worth while to run any risk through mere personal feeling.

At the appointed time, accordingly, the combatants appeared upon the arena at Mars Hill House, in martial array. Messrs. Hunt, Parry, & Co. were led by a lawyer, Mr. Sudlow, whose purpose, it soon appeared, was not to open, but to postpone the battle. I must admit I listened in amazement. Here, after sixteen months of backing and filling, three months after an arbitration had been agreed on, and more than a week after the day had been appointed by them and accepted by me, they apppeared for the purpose of saying that they could not go on with the case. I remembered with astonishment that on the thirteenth of November preceding, the affair had seemed so simple to Mr. Hunt that he had written to one of those friends of mine to whom he had wished and I had declined to refer the case, " If you and I, business men, could have half an hour's talk together, and M. N. would abide by your decision, I think that half hour would be sufficient to settle the whole thing." Whereas, now, before the man whom I had chosen, three months did not seem long enough. The reasons presented by Mr. Sudlow were, first, that the preliminaries were not arranged. The referees themselves averred in substance that this could be done in five minutes on the spot, and there need be no delay on that account.

Mr. Sudlow said, secondly, that at an early stage of the affair I had waived all legal claim, or had never made any, yet that I now appeared with a lawyer as if to establish a legal claim ; that this was an entirely new phase, and one which they could not meet without due preparation. It was alleged in reply, that our courts do not distinguish between legal claims and claims in equity, and that however I might present my claim, it was as a debt and not as a gift; that it surely would not be held by Messrs. Hunt, Parry, & Co., that the reference had been called to arbitrate upon a gratuity. After a good deal of talk, Mr. Dane called for the authority by which they said I had waived all legal claims ; and they produced the letter sent them by me on the 29th August, 1767, about eight months before this time, which said, " Of course I know that legally I have no right to go behind a contract, and therefore no legal claim upon you for additional money on those books that are named in the contract." Mr. Dane pointed out, that, even on this ground there was no waiving of legal claims, except on those books named in the contract referred to. As only three books were embraced in that contract, as one was published under a different contract which we wished carried out, and five were published without any contract at all, the postponing of the case on this pretext was simply preposterous. It seemed to me, moreover, though I said nothing, that even if I had supposed eight months ago that I had no legal claims, I might have subsequently learned otherwise, and that any person who really wanted the case looked into and satisfactorily settled would never have been deterred by so slight an obstacle. But the contest as it stood was two-thirds legal, and it would seem as if an enterprising firm of four shrewd business men might have been prepared to illustrate it in eight months if they had given their minds to it.

Mr. Sudlow affirmed, thirdly, that Messrs. Hunt, Parry, & Co. had supposed they should meet me alone for a friendly reference; that on such a supposition they had arranged to be represented before the referees by one member of their firm, Mr. Markman, who had accordingly prepared to present the case; that until they received Mr. Dane's letter of interrogatories of the 16th instant, they had not supposed I should employ counsel, but if I employed counsel they also should employ counsel; that they were not prepared to appear with counsel, and must have a postponement for the purpose of making such preparation, and as Mr. Hunt was to leave for Europe on the following

Monday, the postponement must hold till after his return from Europe.

Mr. Dane asked them if they meant to allege that they had stipulated that I should not employ counsel. They said they had not so stipulated, but that they supposed I would not employ it. Mr. Dane then said that he had been my adviser from the beginning, both as my friend and as a friend of Mr. Hunt, Mr. Hunt having done him the honor to speak of him as an old friend; that he had had frequent communications with them on this subject, as they well knew, and that they had made no objection to his connection with it; that it made no difference except in name, whether he was called my counsel or my friend; that, although he was a lawyer he trusted he was not on that account to be excluded from the circle of my friends, and that, under the circumstances, it might be proper for him to state that my name had never been on his account-books, and that he had all along counseled me only as a friend. "This thing," he said, "is not to be misunderstood. We want to be definite. Will you say that you will not proceed because M. N. has counsel, — if you choose to call it so, — when she never said that she would not have counsel, nothing ever having been said about it?"

They still reiterated their assertion that under

the circumstances they could not go on with the case. As the business had looked to Mr. Hunt so simple that two business men could settle it in half an hour, it would seem as if almost any kind of a lawyer might have mastered it in the time between the 16th of April, when the idea of my having counsel first dawned upon the unsuspecting minds of Messrs. H., P., & Co., and the 22d, when the hearing was to be had. The firm must rank law far below commerce, if a lawyer could not understand in six days with three men to help him, what a merchant could comprehend in half an hour alone.

Mr. Dane then consulted with me, and I told him upon the impulse of the moment that I would go on. This, perhaps, was hardly prudent or proper. But there had been so much difficulty and delay in bringing things even to this stage, the trouble had weighed so heavily and disastrously upon me, that anything seemed better than an indefinite postponement. Moreover, the reasons which they alleged for delay appeared to me mere quibbles. I thought I saw that they did not design to have any hearing, and that if we should ever get together again, there would be just as much reason for further delay as now, and if I did not secure a hearing now, I never should. I felt that the referees must surely think they had been

summoned on a fool's errand. I was quite aware
not only of my inability to present the case adequately, but to present it at all in person, — but
I had the "brief," which Mr. Dane would have
used, and I had my formidable history in which the
referees could quarry at pleasure. Even if I should
lose the case, I was not without resource ; for upon
the instant when I saw that Messrs. Hunt, Parry,
• & Co. were about to evade the only thing which I
had wanted, namely, a fair and full discussion, there
came into my mind another tribunal which it would
be impossible for them to evade, and before which
I could present my case with or without counsel, in
my own time and way. I had all along had a
vague feeling that something of service to my craft
must come out of all this harassment to me, though
no definite idea had ever evolved itself. But at
that moment, tingling with indignation and con-
tempt, and a sense of outrage, — an outrage greater
than appears here, greater I think than the junior
members of the firm knew or intended, but not
greater than Mr. Hunt knew, and I believe counted
on, — at that moment I resolved that so far as
I could help it, no person should ever be placed in
the position in which I found myself. If any
writer thereafter should get into such a snare, he
should not blunder in as I had done, but walk in
with his eyes open. I thought that my brief and

11

my "Universal History" would be enough to draw the enemy's fire. I should know where they stood, and if I could not understand the analysis and cultivation of the soil, I could at least map out the ground for other investigators. I felt that I could better afford to lose my case than my time. Mr. Hunt had calculated accurately enough the quality and amount of resistance he was accumulating against me. The thing he had not sufficiently calculated was the amount of force that could ·be brought to overcome that resistance.

Mr. Dane then said, that, having consulted me, he had one more proposition to make ; he was not himself surprised at the turn affairs had taken ; he had at the beginning advised me to have recourse to the courts as the only sure way of redress, but that I had always refused to do so ; that he had repeatedly predicted — even to the preceding day — that some way would be found to avoid a hearing ; that he thought it hardly fair for them to force me to go on alone, whom they knew to be entirely unfamiliar with the details of business, who had scarcely in my whole life had any business transactions except with themselves, and had left those entirely in their hands, who had not indeed expected to appear at all in the case, and had only the night before reluctantly consented, at his solicitations, to be present — " If you, gentlemen, think it fair and honorable to insist now, at the last hour, that M. N. shall, without any friend, and entirely unprepared, meet you alone, and conduct the case herself, she will do so. We have come here in good faith to have a hearing, and if such are the only conditions on which it can be had, we will accept them, although I think them hard. We will accept your understanding of the conditions instead of our own. Your firm shall have its representative, I will withdraw, M. N. will do the best she can, and you may see if you can make anything out of it."

Mr. Parry seemed to think, like David Copperfield, that this was a disagreeable way of putting the business, and wished me to state that I did not feel that they wished to take any advantage of me. Mr. Dane said, " I do not know what M. N.'s feelings are. *My* opinion is understood, and I shall state it whenever and wherever I choose."

As my feelings were not under arbitration, I declined, through Mr. Dane, to make any declaration concerning them, but said I wished to go on with the case. Mr. Dane and Mr. Sudlow then withdrew, and the firm were reduced to the painful necessity of proceeding, although their anxiety in regard to my feelings was not relieved.

They did not, however, proceed according to their own statement of what had been their understanding concerning the mode of procedure. Before Messrs. Dane and Sudlow withdrew, Mr. Sudlow said that they were to be represented by one member of their firm, and that Mr. Markman had prepared himself for such representation. Mr. Dane had distinctly stated that he withdrew on this understanding. After he was gone, I expected that Messrs. Hunt & Parry would also withdraw, according to their statement of their original intention, and its acceptance by Mr. Dane. Instead of which, Mr. Parry came to me and asked me if I had any preference as to whether the whole firm should remain or only one member of it. I conceived that this matter had been previously settled by express stipulation, that they had no right to open it again, and place the decision on my preference. I disdained to receive as a favor what seemed to me the least of my rights, and I refused to express any preference about it.

Mr. Parry said, if I had no preference, of course they would rather stay, and they all stayed.

The following paper was then drawn up by the referees and signed by Messrs. Hunt, Parry, & Co. and myself: —

"ATHENS, *April* 22, 1769.

"There being a controversy between Hunt, Parry, & Co., as successors to Brummell & Hunt of Athens, and M. N. of Zoar, in regard to the amount due from the former to the latter for proceeds arising from the publication and sale of the books of which M. N. is the author, it is hereby agreed between the parties to the controversy to submit the points in dispute to George W. Hampden and James Russell, as friendly referees, with the right to the referees to choose a third as umpire, either on the general merits or on any specific point that may be submitted to said third person. And both parties to this agreement hereby bind themselves to accept the award of said referees as binding and conclusive, without reserving any right of appeal to any court of law.

" In witness whereof this agreement is signed by both parties in presence of the referees, to whose custody it is committed."

As I did not intend ever again to sign a paper whose import I did not fully comprehend, it may be supposed that I listened attentively to the reading of this paper. As I had no design to appeal to any court of law, and as it did not preclude me from appealing to the court to which I had made up my mind to appeal, I had no hesitation in signing it.

The case being thus begun, nothing remained but to place in the hands of the referees —

The " entire case in all its bearings" between the firm of Brummell & Hunt and M. N. — as presented by the latter.

Compiled chiefly from the original documents.

In two parts : —

Part First. The case in brief.

Part Second. The case in full.

Each part complete in itself.

The part to be selected according to the taste, object, or judgment of the reader.

October 22, 1768.

THE CASE IN BRIEF.

When Messrs. Brummell & Hunt published " City Lights," they made a contract to pay me ten per cent. on the retail price of the book after the first thousand copies were sold. I did not know that a contract was necessary, but they told me it was, and they also wrote my name in pencil to indicate where I was to write it in ink.

Afterwards they published " Alba Dies " and " Rocks of Offense," without any contract. When " Old Miasmas " was about to be published, it occurred to me that if a contract were necessary in one case, it was in another, and I suggested it to Mr. Hunt. He accordingly had a new contract made out, embracing these three books, in which the firm agreed to pay me fifteen cents a volume for each volume sold. I think it must have been at the time this contract was made out — but I cannot be sure as to the time — that Mr. Hunt told me that they were going to pay me a fixed sum, fifteen cents on a volume, instead of a percentage; that that was the way they were going to do with their authors, on account of fluctuations, general uncertainties, and so forth. I made no objection. I felt none. I assented as a matter of course. I thought that was his business and no affair of mine. I should have thought it intermeddling, and offensive to friendship, to take exception, and I did not dream there was anything to take exception to. I had perfect faith in Mr. Hunt, and reckoned my interests far safer in his hands than in my own.

In the winter of 1767–8, I suddenly awoke to the fact that ten per cent. was the ordinary rate of payment to the author, and that I had been receiving for several years only six and two-thirds and seven and one-half per cent. At the time Mr. Hunt changed his mode of payment, my books were selling at a dollar and fifty cents a volume, so that ten per cent. and fifteen cents were the same. I was therefore the less likely to take exception to the change. The contract embraced "Old Miasmas," which was about to be published, but when it was published the price of it and of the rest of the books was put at two dollars, and has remained so ever since.

All the books that have been published for me by Messrs. H., P., & Co., since "Old Miasmas," have been published without contract. On each of these books, five in number, they have paid me fifteen cents a volume, except "Holidays," on which they paid ten cents a volume. "Holidays" was sold at retail for one dollar and a half; "The Rights of Men" for one dollar and a half; the others were at the price of two dollars. "The Rights of Men" was not published until after I had made objection to the low price I had been receiving.

Pearvilles and Troubadours of Corinth, and publishers of Athens, have told me that ten per cent. on the retail price is the customary pay of authors.

I claim that Messrs. Brummell & Hunt should pay me the difference between what they have paid and what ten per cent. would have been, and that on all books sold in the future, they should pay ten per cent. I agreed to less, in full faith in their uprightness, and in the belief, based on Mr. Hunt's statement, and on my own high opinion of their justice and liberality, that I was faring just as others fared.

Messrs. Brummell & Hunt refuse to pay me more than six and two-thirds and seven and a half per cent. either for the past or the future, except on " The Rights of Men."

To which I had added, February 26, 1769 : —

" I claim now, after fourteen months of what theologians call 'waiting in the use of means,' that they should reimburse me for the time and trouble it has cost me to enforce my claims."

THE CASE IN FULL.

The case in full was the history just given ; compiled, as its perusal shows, from various motives, at various times, for various persons. A few letters between Mr. Dane and myself have been inserted to meet sundry points which afterwards came up. A few slight verbal alterations have been made, and some elegant extracts from the newspapers have been introduced. Otherwise, the statement here made, covering the time from October, 1767, to February, 1769, is the one which was presented to and acted upon by the referees. It was indeed a formidable object, and those unhappy gentlemen may be pardoned if, for a moment, as they held it in their hands, they looked into each other's faces in dismay. But it gives me pleasure to add for the credit of our common humanity, that they met their fate like men, and by a well-organized system of " ride and tie " arrived at their journey's end in a much fresher condition than could have been expected of mere mortals.

When the reading of this document was completed, Messrs. Hunt, Parry, & Co. took up the parable, Mr. Parry being the first spokesman. And here I may say, that notwithstanding their assertion that they had expected to be represented by one of their firm, Mr. Markman, and that on such expectation Mr. Markman had prepared a presentation of the case, when I gave up my arrangements and consented to adopt theirs, their own seemed to have been changed. Instead of one member having it in charge, they all had a share in it, perhaps on the Pauline theory, that if one member suffer, all the members must suffer with him. Mr. Parry began, speaking from notes. Mr. Hunt followed, and Mr. Markman brought up the rear with day-book and ledger. Each one seemed to have his part carefully marked out and assigned to him, and if it had not been for the assertion that they had intended to be represented by one, I should never have suspected that the subsequent management of this case by all three, was a sudden and unaccountable after-thought.

Mr. Parry began by giving a general outline of the trouble as seen from the "Firm" point of sight. He admitted the pleasant relations in which we had previously stood. It seemed that in the latter part of 1767, I had something of a disappointment that the balance due me was not larger, and cast about to see how it could be increased, that the Segregationalissuemost alleged that a larger sum was generally paid than I had received, and Mr. Jackson seemed to confirm this statement; that Mr. Dane, to whom also I had had recourse, had not alleviated my uneasiness, but had rather poisoned my mind against them, as could be seen by the attitude he had assumed here this morning, saying that he had never believed I should have a hearing, and so forth ; that as a result of it all, I considered that I had a claim for additional money, a claim that lay back of the contracts, as I had said ; that I believed they had paid me less than they paid others, and in short brought against them a charge of general disingenuousness.

In replying to Messrs. Hunt, Parry, & Co., I was obliged to omit allusion to sundry points of minor importance, out of a tenderness to the referees — a tenderness of which, probably, until this moment, they had no suspicion. To the readers of this narrative I have no tenderness whatever, since the matter lies in their own hands, and they can dismiss it at pleasure. I shall therefore touch upon various omitted points while sketching the outlines of the defense, and will say here that Mr. Parry's declaration regarding the cause of " The Great Awakening," is strictly true. My eyes were not

opened by any profound reflections on the " Origin
of Evil," or the "Analogy of Religion, Natural
and Revealed, to the Constitution and Course of
Nature," but simply by the ignoble circumstance
that I wanted money in my own miserable purse.
The only consolation to be found for this shameful
disclosure, is the recollection of that three pence a
pound on tea which produced George Washington
and the great American Republic. I have, however, in mitigation of this sordidness, brought forward one or two letters, which show that I wanted
the money for others — the inference naturally being that I was not in so imminent danger of star-
vation that the difference between *meum* and *tuum*
was in my mind entirely obliterated.

Several letters between Mr. Dane and myself
have also been introduced for the purpose of showing to what extent my mind was susceptible of
being poisoned, with what ingredients the attempt
was made, and how far it assimilated and how far
rejected these ingredients. My opinion is, that if
such poisoning be a capital offense, my "attorney"
and myself must die together, for I fear we are
equally guilty.

So far as Mr. Jackson was concerned, Mr. Parry
said that he had been unsuccessful in business, was
not now a regular publisher, and he did not think
his testimony of what was a custom several years

ago was available in deciding what was the custom
now. Regarding Messrs. Troubadour, Pearvilles,
and others, he preserved a discreet silence, but
objected to the introduction of the testimony of
other publishers, as Messrs. H., P., & Co. conducted their business with their authors alone,
without thinking it necessary to consult other publishers. Unless, therefore, I insisted upon other
publishers being brought in, they should prefer to
have them kept out. In reply to a question, Mr.
Parry said he did not know what was the custom
of other publishers in regard to paying authors.
Now it was a very important part of my plan to
have other publishers appealed to, but I was not in
a condition to insist upon anything. I did not
know what to do with them, even if I had them
there. I certainly could not put them through a
catechism, and I had no one to do it for me. So
I said nothing, and the publishers were of course
ruled out — by default, is it ?

Mr. Parry deprecated any attributing of hostility to them. They had been desirous to have
the matter amicably settled, so desirous that they
had even offered to refer it to various friends of my
own, with one of whom they had no acquaintance
at all, with another of whom they had but a slight
acquaintance, but whom they thought competent to
settle it ; and they had also offered to pay me ten

per cent. on all future sales, all of which I had declined.

With regard to the question of fraud, Mr. Parry would say in a general way, that I went to them an unknown author, very urgent to publish "City Lights," that I had a great deal of confidence in them, spoke emphatically of the important advantage to me of being published by Brummell & Hunt; that in short, I came to them in such a way as almost to hold out to them a temptation to defraud me; so that if they had been inclined to it, they would have been likely to do it then. He produced the following extracts from letters written by me to Mr. Hunt, to sustain his charge. And if the printing of these letters seems somewhat appalling, let me assure the objector that it is a pleasing entertainment compared with the sensation of hearing them read before five men, two of whom are indifferent to you, three hostile, and four strangers.

> "Kits, cats, sacks, and wives,
> How many were there going to St. Ives." [1]

I am moved here to say, that those persons who during the present century have been annoyed by letters from this now repentant and remorseful writer, may find ample revenge for all their dis-

---

[1] The editor considers this levity highly unbecoming so solemn an occasion.

comfort in a knowledge of the manner in which these letters have returned to plague the inventor.

The first is dated April 14, 1762.

"I hope this letter sounds light and airy to you. I assure you it is very ghastly joking for me. I am burdened with a terrible secret which I wish to confide to you, at the risk of losing your complaisance forever. I dread to come at it, but I don't see how I can beat about the bush any longer. I am *not* at work on anything for the 'Adriatic.' You would not print my papers, and you would not answer my letters. So Satan subsidized my idle hands, and I thought I would make a book. So I *made* a book. It is not about the war, nor the times, nor anything sensible. It is not a novel, nor a history, nor a poem, nor a criticism, nor a volume of sermons. Somehow it does not look like a book, nor sound like a book, nor act like a book, but it *is* a book. I can make 'my davy' on that. There is a title and a place for a preface, and an introduction, and I can put in an appendix if I wish, and explanatory notes and a glossary, and errata, and if you will publish it I will give you the copyright and the premium, and the patent, and the monopoly, and all the dividends, and if there is anything else, that — its title is 'City Lights.' It is blocked out in twelve chapters.

" ' 1. Moving ' — That gets us out of the old house into the new one, and gives us a local habitation and a starting-point. I wrote it for the A. M. but you stunned me so with hurling back my paper pellets at my head that I did not dare try it again.

" ' 2. The Bank '— That means a grass bank, not a money bank. That has been printed.

" ' 3. My Garden ' — That you have heard of. That was what I wanted the proof-sheets for, and you may conceive how guilty I felt. It seemed all the while like when Joab said to Amasa, ' Art thou in health, my brother? ' and took him by the beard with the right hand to kiss him, and smote him under the fifth rib, — the wretch! But you see I was forced to be wily. If you had known that I was conspiring against your peace of mind, of course you would not have put the weapon into my hand. So I had to take you by the beard tenderly, or I should not have got the fifth rib at all, and that is the backbone of my book.

" ' 4. Men and Women ' — Been printed.

" ' 5. Tommy ' — Been printed.

" ' 6. Boston and home again ' — Been printed — personal adventures of a rustic in the city.

" ' 7. Friendship ' — In your hands — will be when you get this.

" ' 8. Dog-days ' — Been printed.

" ' 9. Fading as a leaf ' — Or something of that

sort — knocks the bottom all out of the autumnal, sentimental kind of moral reflections — been printed.

" ' 10. Winter ' — Snow and coal-fires — been printed.

" ' 11. My Flower-bed ' — A success, to offset the failure to ' My Garden.'

" ' 12. Happiest Days.'

" Now, the question is, will you let me send it to you ? You see it is almost all in print, so it will take but a minute to run it over — a longish kind of a minute, of course. I have not the least idea whether it is worth publishing or not. I don't want it published unless it will reflect credit on the literature of the country. Now, may I be forgiven for telling a lie ; but I don't want it published if it will reflect *dis*credit — I will stick to that. I don't want it published unless it will be read and liked by cultivated people. I don't want it to be at the level of school-girls and shop-boys. I want it to be such a book as ——— or ——— or ——— or ——— or ——— might take into the country, not for the thought or the theory, but for amusement, and such as would amuse them ; such as Englishmen might read and value for its little side-lights thrown on American country life. I don't aim to do anything above amusement, and if it wont do that it is a failure, for there is nothing

12

else for it to do. You see it was not written with any view to a book. I suppose I have enough things printed to make a dozen books, and I have taken out enough for one about the size of ' Sir Thomas Browne.' So far as the people I write for are concerned, I think now is as good a time as any. There is a kind of hiatus in book-making, and that gives me a chance for a hearing. My audience is more at leisure now and not much poorer. It is specially adapted to the times in that it has not anything to do with them, and so will be a recreation if it is not a bore. I should not think it would sell, I must say, for there is not anything of it. Still, all the parts of it that have been printed have ' taken ' — I don't understand why. . . . .

" I have a certain vivacity of style which would be well enough if I had anything solid underneath ; but I have no thought, no depth, no severe and careful culture, no comprehensiveness, no substance, nothing to raise me above the penny-a-liners, except perhaps the matter of vivacity, or whatever it is — but that is nothing to depend upon — no resource, no capital. My chief talent consists in raising great expectations — which will turn out like Pip's, I expect. It is no fault of mine. I do conscientiously the best I can ; you are an illustration of this thing. You expect ' A number one ' things of me. But you have no ground for it. I have sent you

my ' A number one ' things already, and you see
they are not ' up to the mark.' But they are the
very best I can do under the circumstances. What
right have you then to expect anything better? I
consider it a great misfortune that somehow my
performances seem to give a promise that is entirely
unwarrantable. O well, I must stop some time, so
I suppose I might as well stop here. All is, may
I send the thing to you? It is all ready, only I
have to take it to some book-binder somewhere to
have the things pasted in. I hope I do not annoy
you by asking you — not *much* I mean ; of course
it must annoy you a little — I assure you you need
not have the slightest feeling about saying *no*. It
would be no kindness to me to suffer me to disgrace
myself or my country. There is only one sin that
I will never forgive. If you ever tell anybody,
my wrath will kindle against you into a perpetual
fire ; and you know about furies, and scorned
women, and the wicked place! I hope this will
get at you in some little crack between two ' *mad* '-
nesses, but if it does not, pray don't turn ' mad ' at
me. I can bear anything but to be snapped up. I
wonder if you would be more likely to be pleased if
I had stopped before ; if so, you can just turn back
to the place where your temper began to crack,
and make believe ' Yours, respectfully,' came there.
But you have been so generous hitherto that I am

afraid I perhaps presume too far — now I am sure
that compliment is very well turned, seeing that
kind of thing is not in my line — but the fact is I
want you to stay good-humored so much that I
would say anything!

Yours very truly,   M. N."

The letters from Mr. Hunt in reply to mine, are
inserted here for a better understanding of my letters, and to preserve the unity of the drama.   As
I did not anticipate the appearance of mine before the referees, Mr. Hunt's were not arranged
with reference to them, but have been placed here
since.   Several sentences concerning magazine
articles are quoted, to show that though I had not
printed a book I was not wholly unknown as an
author at the time of the publication of " City
Lights," and that therefore the risk was not quite
so great as one would perhaps judge from Mr. Parry's statement, which will presently appear.

MR. HUNT TO M. N.

" Send along the book by all means, and I will
give it early attention. . . . . A *book* from your
hand is worthy attention, and it shall have it from
yours truly."

APRIL 20, 1762.

" I have read 'Moving' and the 'Friendship' paper to-day, both of which I shall be glad to print in the Magazine if you will let me. . . . . As soon as I can find more time I will make up my mind about the book."

APRIL 25, 1762.

" I wish to begin at once to set up the copy, and no time should be lost in waiting. October will soon be here !

" I think we shall be able to get into a volume your articles, in form like 'Old Sir Thomas.' At any rate I shall try to do so."

APRIL 29.

" Why do you hop about so when you attempt an epistle ? I can't find the place. Now you are on the right side of a sheet, and, *presto !* I can't tell next where you are. A reader of your letters ought to stand on his head half the time. Page two is nowhere to be found, without twisting the spinal apparatus fearfully. Why don't you have a plan and stick to it ? Or are you a law unto yourself ? (See Hebrews).

" Let me tell you what I would like to do : Print in the Magazine several of the articles in your proposed volume, postponing the publication in book

form for the present. 'Moving,' and ' Friends and
Friendship,' I certainly wish for the Magazine. . . . .
. . . . Your book will keep, wont it? Meantime
the papers, as printed in the "Adriatic," will not
badly advertise the coming volume. Do you agree
with me? . . . .

" Your 'My Garden,' is a hit number one.
Crowds of inquiries for the author's name beseech
me, but I cry ' *mum*' to the myriads."

"Can't you read figures, dear? Don't you know
a five when you see it? Aren't you able to tell a
two from a four unless they are labelled? I fondly
believed you were, but as indications point the
other way, I will have everything in a right line
hereafter, so that I shall just have to drop you into
the groove at the beginning and you will spin along
of yourself to the end. I am your serf and slave
— till I get the upper hands of you, which I shall
one day — I always do, sooner or later. Don't be
frightened, though. I shall roar you as gently as a
sucking-dove. And please remember that Hebrews
is not Romans — or, as one cannot remember what
he never knew, please be informed. Aren't you
glad you have somebody who can always set you
right?

" There is one thing about my letters though;—

when you do find the place you know where you
are. Yours I don't. Now what do you mean?
Do you mean that my book is not good enough to
publish? If you do, why don't you say so?

" When I was in Congress anything that was in-
definitely postponed was as good as lost. I wish
you would say, straight as an arrow, just what you
mean. You need not be afraid of wounding my
feelings. I have boxed them up in ice and saw-
dust and set them on the top shelf till such time as
my fortunes shall permit me to indulge in such
luxuries. I am rhinocerine and pachydermatous.
Lay on Macbeth, or Duff, or whoever you are.

" You see it is absurd for you to talk about postponing the publication of a general kind of book if
it is worth publicating at all. If it were what I
want it to be, you would rectangle it up in ten minutes and have it out. If it is not what I want it to
be, I don't want it published at all. If it is only
so-so, pay-the-way-y, very good, I will have none
of it. I want it to be triumphantly good. I
don't want any drawn battle. I want an uncondi-
tional surrender, with fort, guns, and ammunition.
If I can't have that I don't want anything. Now
can I have that? You tell me. I know you know.
I have been flattered to death all my life. . . .
If the book is coarse, and violent, and insipid, and
diffuse, and superficial, and egotistical, and worth-

less, say so.   That is just what I am afraid it is,
and it keeps me awake nights.

"It occurs to me that possibly you may have so
much on your hands that you cannot publish it.   I
don't believe that, though.   People can always find
time to do what they will to do, — any way I can,
and I am a female Atlas.   But if it were so, and
you would tell me that you thought the book was
good, I would get somebody else to publish it.   I
should not like to do it to be sure.   I have set my
heart on your publishing my first book.   You see,
as Mrs. Browning says, 'I love high though I live
low.'   You know if you aim at the sun you won't
probably hit it, but you will hit higher than you
would if you made your target out of a scrub
oak.   I don't want to go into the world through
the back door.   I want to go in, sir, by the main
entrance! with drums beating and colors flying!
with body-guard on each side, and carriages drawn
up in line!   That means you — Brummell & Hunt
is the triumphal arch and the Seventh Regiment!
But you see I am tired to death and disgust of
waiting.   It is three years now since I took to writing in good earnest, and all this while I have been
burrowing under ground.   It is almost two years
since I sent 'My Garden' to the 'A. M.'   Two years
apiece for the other two things will be four years,
and by that time I shall be a coral reef, with all the

pulp of my soul dried up, and nothing left but the dead shell. You understand I am not impatient of preparation. I am not only willing but eager to work. If I thought I could be more worthy by waiting; if I thought crudeness would mellow, I would wait; but the book is done. It is not a question of improving it, but to be or not to be.

"It would be a great disappointment, and I am sure a positive loss to me, not to have you publish the book if it is fit to publish. You would give me a prestige which I assure you I have sense enough to value. And yet will not the book, if it is good, make its own way, even if it should be born in a garret? You see I look at this from my standing-point only, for you of course are too well established to be disgraced by my failure or illustrated by my success. I am the only one affected, don't you see? If I fail it will nerve me. If I succeed it will give me a point of support. You understand, by success I don't mean that I desire to make a sensation. The public, whose countenance I court, would be comprised in a hundred men and women. If I should secure their suffrage, the rest of the world might go whistle. If the hundred put me on the pedestal, the ten millions cannot pull me down, for it is quality and not quantity that leads in this world, no matter what the world thinks.

"I want to be out too, because that thing is only the inch of an ell. If that succeeds I have half a dozen others — 'City Lights,' — in the same style — and 'Rocks of Offense,' which is to put everybody right in religious matters. You don't know what my prophetic style is? I tell you it leaves Isaiah and Jeremiah nowhere! Then there is 'Night Caps' for children, and 'Holiday Stories' for all the holidays, and 'Stories of the Old School-House,' etc. I have sent those to the Tract Society and all the Eleemosynary Institutions, but they were not considered pious enough, and I am afraid you profane establishments would think they were too pious, so betwixt the clergy and the laity I should come to the ground with a thud, from which, like Antæus, I always gather strength.

"I don't believe you half read my letters. I don't know that I blame you, but it leads you into obvious mistakes. You say you want to print several of the articles — two certainly. Goosey-goosey-gander, where shall I wander; did not I tell you that all but those two had been printed before, and the last one which you had rejected? Why do you talk? . . . . I am going to Athens to buy a new dress the first pleasant day of next week after Monday. Would you be willing to send those two papers around to —— ? I can look them over and manipulate them, and return them the next day. If you obey the impulse of the natural heart, unmodified by pressure of editorial duties, you will tell me, as General Taylor told Santa Anna, ' Come and take them.' And I would be glad to do it and talk about these matters instead of writing. But you must know that I cannot talk — I say what I don't mean and I mean what I don't say, and so an interview would be entirely inconclusive and unsatisfactory.

" You will understand from this brief epistle that it is not the book that won't keep so much as it is my own self.

" If I have said anything here that I ought not to say, pray make believe that — there, I just remember that my little book is not ' Night-Caps ' but ' Make-Believes ' — there is a book ' Night-Caps already. Well, what I was going to say is — make believe I have not said it. I am writing in greatest stress of time, for our mail goes at unearthly hours, and I cannot stop to be proper. I wish you would give me a general absolution, retro- and pro-spective, till this business is over. Yours very truly.

MR. HUNT TO M. N.

" I see we must speak by the card when we write to Miss Wont-understand.

" This then, is what I wished to say in my last clear and felicitous epistle.

" Of course your book cannot be published till the articles I propose to print in the A. M. have appeared there. This is what I meant by postponing the issue of the volume. I wished to say that, B. & H. would print your book, certainly, but the time when must at present be unsettled for the reason above given. I have read the articles now and like them hugely. They are capital stuff for a book, full of all readable qualities. . . . .

" I will not eat you if you call in here when you come to town, but you must have your own way."

All the confidence, and all the respect for the house of Brummell & Hunt, which these letters indicate, I not only admit, but I introduced my case by avowing that I thought them the head and front of all publishing houses.

With regard to the exemption of fifteen hundred as the first edition of " City Lights," Mr. Parry said that the word edition meant nothing as to number. It meant simply a single issue. In reply to a question, he said he did not know what was the usage of publishers in this regard. They had sometimes exempted as many as two thousand, and had known cases in which five thousand had been exempted, and, I understood him to say, had done it themselves. One thousand, he said, was the usual number. Being asked what would be his own understanding of an edition, if nothing were specified, he said he would frankly admit that he should suppose it meant one thousand; that when any larger number than a thousand was exempted, it was their custom always to specify the number; that he did not know why it was not done now, and presumed this was the only time they had exempted more than a thousand without specifying the number. The reason of this large exemption was that there was so much risk in publishing a new book, and that this book was published in a style that was unusually expensive. It cost a great deal more than any other on their list; that there was no prescribed usage in such matters, and they could have exempted more, but had no desire to do so. I had said that if it were to cost more, they should have told me.[1] They had letters of mine showing that I did know it cost more, but that I was so desirous to have it printed in this way, that, in my own language, which Mr. Markman read and Mr. Hunt repeated with an air which showed that whatever literature had gained, the stage lost its chief ornament when Mr. Hunt

---

[1] I think this matter in detail came up subsequently in connection with the diminished price paid me for copyright, but as it belongs here also, I put it in all at once.

went into the book trade, "I went down on my knees to you to have it like Sir Thomas Browne."

In my original statement I had said, "When the first book was to be published, Mr. Hunt asked me what style I should like, and suggested that of the 'City Curate.' I preferred 'Sir Thomas Browne.' He made no objection, nor even hinted that it was more expensive than the other. [Then came the quotations.] "I do not recollect that anything was said about it afterwards. The following books were simply published in uniform style with the first." This is my recollection of the matter, which is simple and commonplace enough.

From my letters at the time, however, the firm of Brummell & Hunt infer a thrilling dramatic scene in which Mr. Hunt was the obdurate autocrat, or the wise and thrifty guardian, as the case may be, who, like Mrs. John Gilpin, though on publishing bent, had a frugal mind; but was at length moved by me,

> " Languendo, gemendo
> Et genuflectendo,"

to lay aside prudence and launch out into a style of publication which could be met only by some extraordinary sacrifice on my part, I professing to be until this late disclosure ignorant both of style and sacrifice.

I give the correspondence, inserting Mr. Hunt's

letters to throw light on mine — the latter only appearing in Mr. Parry's defense.

Let it be remembered that the book was published September 18, 1762.

MR. HUNT TO M. N., SEPT. 2, 1762.

" It is our intention to publish ' C. L.,' on Saturday, the 13th of this month : not before, certainly. If any great excitement befall the country, we shall postpone till the following Saturday. . . .

" Your new preface is pungent as a pepper. Your motto seems to be, ' Je suis prêt.'

" Give it to 'em any way you like. A proof of the preface will go to you in a few days. As to the binding of your book, I propose same style as ' Rs. of a City Curate,' gilt top leaves and beveled boards. Do you like that way ? "

M. N. TO MR. HUNT, SEPTEMBER 3.

" For you to set up and pretend to ask me if I like ' City Curate ' style, when you knew I went down on my knees to you to have it like ' Sir Thomas Browne,' and you said you would.

" The next book you publish for me, I am going to stand over you with a grip on your coat-collar from the time you give the first copy to the printer till the first edition stands on the shelf, and see if you cannot be kept to something. I don't know

what your beveled boards are — only if you put a
d in, the adjective would apply more accurately —
and I don't want my book to be boarded up any
way, and if there is anything I hate, it is gilt tops,
and if you don't do it as I want it, I don't care how
it is done."

MR. HUNT TO M. N., SEPTEMBER 15.

"We shall publish, unless a defeat crowns our
victories, your book this week. It will be a beauty,
and look like "Sir Thomas Browne,' in its red
waistcoat."

[This letter was delayed and not received till
the following letter was partly written.]

M. N. TO MR. HUNT, SEPTEMBER 20, 1762.

"You darling Traddles, — why do I call you
Traddles? Because you are 'the dearest fellow.'
It was not Traddles, though, was it? It was his
wife, and she was not a fellow but a girl — never
mind. The fact I wish to impress upon your mind
is, that you have tricked out my book so beautifully
that nothing could be lovelier. You would not
have done it though if I had not threatened you
within an inch of your life, would you? You
don't know how delighted I was when I opened
the bundle, expecting to see those cheap-looking

paste-boardy things, and you had gone and done them just as I wanted you to do them, and you said you would, and then said you wouldn't, and they are *beautiful*. They are better even than 'Sir Thomas.' The paper is' finer. But now see — I never thought till yesterday that they must cost more than the other way, and I have been distressed all along, and this makes me more so. But listen : I shall either live, or die, or marry. If I live I shall get money, if not by writing, then by teaching, or something, so that I shall pay you sometime. If I die I shall leave money enough of my own to pay you, and you keep this letter to show to my heirs to let them know I desire you to be paid. If I marry, Smith of course will be delighted to pay all my debts, and I shall make that the condition of my becoming Smithess ; so that you shall not *lose* money on my book, even if you don't make any, which I hope you will — millions of dollars; but I am sure you must see for yourself that it is better to have a book look substantial and high-bred, and suit you, even if it does cost a little more.

" Just here comes your letter and check, which was delayed in Boston because you did not put a stamp on.

" One of my friends has been questioning me about the business part of my book — copyrights

13

and contract, and all that trash of which I know and care nothing."

[Foolish as this all seems to me now, I can only say that it expressed exactly my state of mind. It was not that I had any lofty disregard of money, but simply that I was so intent on writing, that I had room for nothing else. I had plenty of money, or if I had not, I did not know it, which amounts to the same thing, and it made me impatient to be bothered with these outside, and what seemed to me entirely insignificant matters.]

"But I want to know if by publishing articles in the 'A. M.' they pass out of my hands. I mean, if I wanted to collect them and have Tilton, say, publish them, couldn't I? I will any way; because you see, though *I* am amiable, you know what *your* temper is, and suppose we flare up and have a quarrel, what then? I tell you I don't discard lines of retreat. Now you know I would rather have you publish than anybody else — supposing I had anything to be published; but I want to do it because I want to do it, and not because I *have* to do it — don't you understand?

"Do you know that it scares me to see my book out in the open day? Seems to me it is a romping kind of a book, and there is a regiment of I's on every page, and 'lots' of 'tricksys' and 'exasperatings' and 'for my parts.' You cannot tell

how a book will look till it is born, can you? I
shall make the next one better. Shall you read
it now it is out? I wish I knew whether it dis-
appoints you. It does me. It is crude and botchy
— it is so awfully unlike ' Sir Thomas Browne ; '
and if it *isn't* good, it is frightfully pretentious. A
book ought not to come out in that style, unless
it has some merit. To think of —— reading it,
and —— and —— and —— I should like to go
into a hole and burrow — and ——

"O dear! I don't suppose they will read it, but
I wanted to have such a book as they will read.
Any way, you have done your part, and I want
you to know that I am aware of it and not ungrateful."

"Hurrah! Good news! I have heard of a
man in S——, who *said* he was *going* to buy my
my book! There is one copy as good as sold.

"The man who told me about the purchaser in
S——, tells me also that the dress of my book is
very much admired, and says I ought to be very
grateful to B. & H. for doing me up in such style,
just as if I was not! But what can I do about it?
There is a white cloud at the toe of my boot. As
soon as it resolves itself into a well-defined hole, I
am coming to Athens to get a new pair. I have
nothing in the world to say to you, and I shall not
come to see you. Still, if you should say, ' Hadn't

you better?' perhaps I might be induced to rasp
my knuckles against No. 7—."

MR. HUNT TO M. N., SEPTEMBER 23.

" I am glad you like the costume into which we
put your first-born. It is a handsome baby and
will go alone uncommonly early."

So it seems that notwithstanding all the impor-
tunities and posturings of the kneeling scene, Mr.
Hunt was unmoved — for it was after the curtain
had fallen on this act that he quietly writes, " I
propose same style as 'City Curate.' Do you like
it?" All its pathos had not been sufficient to keep
the act itself in mind. When I first suggested
" Sir Thomas Browne," he agreed at once, but afterwards apparently forgot it and mentioned " City
Curate," as if nothing had before been said on the
subject. Finding then that I wanted the " Sir
Thomas," he does not so much as reply, but simply
binds the book according to my wishes. There is
no sign of any objection to it on his part from the
beginning to the end, so that the candid inquirer
is at a loss to know why I should have knelt, except from native humility of spirit and taste for the
suppliant posture — which nobody can deny.

As the ministers remark, " we shall resume this
subject in the afternoon's discourse." I only say

here what, *à la* Ollendorf's grammar, I had a mind
but no time to say to the referees.

After we had all slept upon it and returned to
our *moutons* next morning, Messrs. Hunt, Parry, &
Co. brought in proof to show that I did know that
fifteen hundred books were exempted in the first
edition. This was an account in one of their books
in which the exemption appeared. But in their
copy of the accounts sent to me, drawn up by their
clerk for the referees, the latter remarked that no
such item appeared. Messrs. Parry and Markman
thought it might be the clerk's mistake in copying.
The referees asked me if I had my accounts with
me. As they had been my literature for sixteen
months, I was inclined to think I had. The original papers were produced and no mention was found
in them of any exempted copies. Mr. Parry said
that as the item was down in the books it must have
been put there for the purpose of sending to me.
Mr. Markman thought this particular account might
have been lost in the mail. But the accounts which
I held covered all the time of my transactions with
Messrs. B. & H. Mr. Parry thought the entry in
their books would at least show their good intentions.

The second edition of "City Lights" numbered
five hundred copies. No edition was so large as
the first, except the eleventh, which numbered two

thousand copies. Another fact came out of which I had not before been aware, that three hundred copies had been exempted on every book. These I suppose had been distributed as advertisements.

Regarding the change in payments from percentage to a fixed sum, the firm claimed that it was made with my full knowledge, understanding, and consent, as would be proved by Mr. Hunt's testimony. Whereupon Mr. Parry gave place to Mr. Hunt, who deposed and said — or rather, to his grief, did not depose, but was obliged to content himself with saying, — that on a certain time he held a long conversation with me on the subject of the change, in which he fully explained to me its nature and necessity. He remembered that at first I was disposed to be trifling, but he begged that I would be serious, and assured me that this was a serious matter. He remembered using the expression, that their house was shaking in the wind. He explained to me over and over again, to make sure that I understood the state of affairs and the reasons which necessitated the change, and repeatedly asked me, " Do you understand this clearly ? " and I said that I did, and " Do you assent to it ? " and I answered " Yes." Then, fastening upon me a look — apparently designed to be penetrating and powerful enough to reach the lowest depths of duplicity and to wring late confession even from a perjured soul,

—he exclaimed, "I think, M. N., you *must* remember this."

Of course I was overwhelmed with confusion, but having persisted in the falsehood so long it was hardly worth while to go down on my knees to the gentleman a second time, so I received his gaze in silence. In fact, Mars Hill House witnessed then what the hymn calls "the young dawn of heaven below," inasmuch as there was silence in the room for the space of not quite half an hour. It was broken by the referees, who said that it was perhaps proper to ask me here if I remembered any such conversation. I said that I did not recollect it. They asked Mr. Hunt if he had any correspondence which referred to it. He said no, only the letter of mine which I had myself produced, in which I admitted it. But he remembered it with exact clearness. He could recall just the sofa on which he sat. He was so confident that he wished he could take his oath on it. They asked him whether I happened to be in Athens or whether he sent for me. He was not sure, but thought he sent for me. They asked him if in this conversation it was understood that "City Lights" was to be included in the second contract. He said "distinctly." I asked if he could define the time when the conversation occurred. He could not, but it was some time before the second contract was made, and was the basis of that contract. I asked if he could tell whether it was in the old shop or the new. He said it was in the new. He did *not* add, what would have been a most effective peroration to his speech, —

"I reside at Table Mountain, and my name is Truthful James;
I am not up to small deceit or any sinful games."

This little matter being thus comfortably disposed of, Mr. Parry again took up the thread of his discourse.

With regard to the change in payment to authors from a percentage to a fixed sum, he said that such a change was desirable because everything was changing and uncertain. He reiterated his statement as to the variations that had been made in the retail price of my books; said that authors generally did accede to the change; admitted that Mrs. ——— had had some difficulty, that her mind seemed to have been jaundiced towards them, that her sister, Miss ———, had examined their books, and that Mrs. ——— had now become satisfied that all was right; that I, before the reference, neither admitted nor denied that I had acceded to their proposal, but only affirmed that I did not recollect about it. He denied that there was any prescriptive custom of paying the author ten per cent., though as before, he objected to bringing in the modes of other publishers, as Hunt, Parry, & Co.

transacted business on their own account without consulting others. Which is all very true, doubtless, yet the prejudiced observer, seeing how much is said about the great liberality of this firm, can but marvel that they should have been willing to miss so brilliant an opportunity of contrasting their own liberality with the niggardliness of those sordid book-men who publish, not for glory and high emprise, but simply to make money. Mr. Parry said this also was a reason why the questions propounded to them by Mr. Dane antecedent to the reference seemed irrelevant. They were asked to state their income and that from the "Adriatic." But they might make a great deal of money in outside ways, — by speculating in butter, for instance,— of which it was not pertinent that they should give any account. He was asked why, if there was no prescribed custom to pay ten per cent., they themselves fixed on ten per cent. as the rate of payment for "City Lights." He said that they were disposed to be liberal ; that there were no fluctuations then ; that such a prescriptive custom may then have existed, he would not say that ten per cent. was not common, though he did not himself know what was the custom among other publishers. He was asked why "City Lights" was not by name included in the second contract if its provisions were intended to apply to "City Lights," and why the

other works were not also included in a contract.
He replied, that it was because a verbal understanding had been reached; that if they had supposed
or intended any wrong, they would certainly have
so included it; that the absence of contracts was
owing to a basis of mutual understanding and verbal agreements. He was asked if they had any
letters bearing on such verbal agreements, and he
said they had not.

He affirmed that the publishers made but insignificant profits on the books compared with mine;
that up to September, 1764, when the second contract was made, when "City Lights" had been
two years out and "Alba Dies" and "Rocks of Offense" had been published, and "Old Miasmas"
was about to be published, their net cash profit on
the books for these two years had been three hundred dollars. Here they went into the details of the
business with a minuteness altogether beyond my
power to comprehend or report. The referees and
themselves carried on a long discussion about the
condition of business in general, and their business
in particular, in 1762, 1764, and subsequently. The
firm foresaw that they should have to advance the
retail price of their books. Everything connected
with their business advanced. The price and quality of paper, the size of books, taxes, interest,
stereotype plates, pro rata increase, press-work,

expenses of business, comparative costs of comparative thinness, if there is any such thing, number of pounds of paper in thin books and thick books, discounts to the trade, were discussed with apparent intelligence.   I can give only a few of the mysterious tongues of flames that shot above the level of the luminous, and still more mysterious corona.

[It will be seen that this part of my paper is like Milton's " fatal and perfidious bark," in " being built in the eclipse" as well as "rigged with curses dark."]

The stereotype plates of the nine volumes were estimated at three thousand nine hundred and fifty-three dollars, ninety-seven cents.

Paper, printing, and binding of about 72,000 volumes	$38,422.08
Advertising in outside mediums .	1,500.00
Advertising in their own periodicals	500.00

[The latter embraced only *cost* of paper and printing.]

Government manufacturing tax, five per cent. on sales, October 1764 to July 1766	$1,814.04
Seven per cent. interest on stereotype plates	991.46
Expenses of doing business, ten per cent. on sales	7,061.14

The latter included rent, insurance, clerk hire, packing, store expenses, business risks and losses, taxes on business-property, except income-tax, etc. Reckoning up the sums expended they proved beyond doubt, if there be truth in figures, that their profits were not quite seven-tenths as large as those of the opulent and insatiable author, who, in spite of all this inequality.was clamoring for more. But they admitted that, though their expenses had been out of all proportion to their profits since the rise in prices, their profits had lately " been *some* larger than before."

With all due respect to Messrs. Hunt, Parry, & Co., I must still avow that these estimates are entirely valueless. What would have been of value was their cost-book, which would have showed what they actually did pay. This I asked for but it was not produced. They simply made an estimate. They brought forward not a single voucher. They reckon the item of advertising at two thousand dollars, but they produced not a paper to show that they had paid anything. This advertising extended over several years and embraced advertisements of nine books. Whether they counted in the three hundred volumes reserved on each book ; whether they counted in the advertisements of every book advertised and issued simultaneously with mine, on what basis they did calculate, or what sums they did pay, I have no means of knowing, except their assertion.

In the same way they make their estimate of the cost of paper and press-work; but that it is anything more than an estimate, that it represents the actual sum which they paid to printers and binders, there is no proof. From the fact that I asked for their cost-book, and that it was not produced, I infer that it does not represent that sum, notwithstanding the laudable accuracy involved in the eight cents.

Again, having set down a certain sum for the cost of the stereotype plates, for the interest of that money, for the paper and press-work, for the advertising and taxes, they bring in a grand finale for the expenses of doing business. That is, having charged once for the items specifically, they lump them together and charge for them all over again abstractly. For what is the advertising and the taxes but a part of the expenses of doing business? Why could not everything except the raw material of the book be classed under the head of doing business? What is there to a book but the book itself and the publication of it? And why again should interest be charged on the sum paid for stereotype plates any more than for that paid to the printer and binder?

[Since the reference I have showed their state-

ment to several publishers, and am assured that any
person whose correct accounts should stand thus
is unfit for the business, and that the profit on those
books is from four to five times as much as Messrs.
Hunt, Parry, & Co. represent it.]

But, even supposing all these figures to be correct, it will at once be seen that the publishers set
off their own net profits against the author's gross
receipts. Having charged for every item of their
own expense in producing the book, and for some
of them twice over, they make no allowance whatever for the author's having been at any expense in
his part of the production. What the publisher gets
after every expense is paid is set over against what
the author gets to pay every expense with. But
the publisher's profits, according to their showing,
are only about one tenth of his gross receipts. What
then is the author's share of what may truly be
termed profits? Or is the author's share in the
production of the book to be considered as of no
pecuniary value?

The remainder of the case, as presented by
Messrs. Hunt, Parry, & Co., will appear, to the
best of my ability, in the written reply presented
to the referees and here subjoined. It must not be
forgotten that one is always liable to misrepresent
an opponent's case. I labor under the additional
disadvantage of possessing a natural aptitude for

" conspicuous inexactness " perfected by long practice. This innate depravity is, however, held in
check at the present crisis, by the consciousness
that I am reporting what took place in the
presence of five persons, of whom three were on
the other side, and two on neither side, so that
any lapse from truth would be speedily detected.
With such vigor does Providence barricade our
weaker virtues !

INTRODUCTION.

(This " Introduction " will doubtless induce in
the reader a despair akin to that felt by a sleepy
worshipper on a warm Sunday afternoon, when,
nearing, as he supposes, the close of the discourse,
the preacher turns over a new leaf, and announces,
" Secondly ! ")

" INTRODUCTION.

" Before proceeding to the subject-matter of the
controversy, will the referees permit me to apologize for appearing before them to present the case
myself. Nothing was further from my intention.
Until the evening before the reference I did not
mean to be present at all, and I then consented to
be in the room only at Mr. Dane's urgent solicita-
tion. I wished a full, clear, and exhaustive discussion. I knew that I was not able to enter into

it myself. I have steadfastly refused to attempt it
even in private with Messrs. Hunt and Parry, because I knew I was so ignorant of the details of
business, that such a discussion would be fruitless.
How much less then should I have attempted it
before two gentlemen of the character and ability
of the referees, appealed to for a formal and final
decision ?

" The paper already presented to the referees was
prepared originally for my own convenience, and
was subsequently put into Mr. Dane's hands for his
exact understanding of the matter. It was not
designed for the referees. It contained much irrelevant matter, and my only excuse for offering it,
is the embarrassment and perplexity in which I
suddenly found myself involved, and from which
this seemed the only way of escape.

" The same circumstances must be my apology to
Mr. Hunt for certain letters which appeared in that
statement. They were placed there only for the
sake of a few lines which were in them. These
extracts were all that were designed to be read.
But in the confusion of the moment I was entirely
unable to make any separation or distinction. I
mention this, not because the letters contained
anything discreditable to Mr. Hunt, for they did
not ; but because I would wish to avoid even the

appearance of unnecessarily giving private letters to the semi-publicity of arbitration.[1]

" For the paper which I now present, I must also beg the indulgence of the referees. I have done the best I could do under the circumstances, but I know that it must seem to them redundant, deficient, unsystematic, and perhaps inadequate. I can only assure them that had I thought it possible I should be forced to conduct the case myself, I should never have appealed to arbitration.

" I beg to thank the referees most sincerely for their unvarying kindness and forbearance.

" SUBJECT—MATTER OF THE CONTROVERSY.

" I claim what is justly due for copyright on eight works, namely : —

" ' City Lights,'
" ' Alba Dies,'
" ' Rocks of Offense,'
" ' Old Miasmas,'
" ' Pencillings,'
" ' Holidays,'
" ' Cotton-Picking,'
" ' Winter Work,'

Published by Messrs. Brummell & Hunt, since Hunt, Parry, & Co.

" Were there no contracts, the author's share

---

[1] These letters do not appear in this publication.

14

should, I suppose, be determined by the usage of publishers and authors, as to similar works with similar sales.

" For four of these books there is no contract.

" On the first book, ' City Lights,' there is a written contract at ten per cent. on the retail price after the first edition is sold. This price was fixed voluntarily by the publishers without suggestion from or consultation with me, and must be considered as expressing their idea of what was fair and usual under ordinary circumstances, even with a new author. This contract has never been rescinded. Messrs. Hunt, Parry, & Co. claim that it has been rescinded. No one can be called upon to prove a negative. To prove that the contract exists, I produce the contract. To prove that the rescission exists, I demand that they produce the rescission. This they have utterly failed to do. Mr. Hunt simply asserts a verbal agreement, which I deny. A verbal agreement between two parties, which one party stoutly maintains, and the other flatly denies, is, I submit, an agreement more suited to the latitude and longitude of Dublin than of Athens. A verbal agreement, which on examination proves to be an utter and absolute disagreement, cannot cancel a written contract.

" They not only attempt to rescind the first contract, but to substitute another for it by including

'City Lights' in the second contract. But 'City Lights' is not named in the second contract. They do not even pretend that they intended to name it there. They simply assert a conversation in which both parties agreed that, the first contract still existing, they would act as if it did not exist; and that 'City Lights' not being inserted in the second contract, both parties should act as if it were so inserted. I beg to inquire if there is anything in the Union as it was, or the Constitution as it is, that could make such a procedure reasonable? Is it credible that a shrewd business firm should rely on a verbal agreement to cancel a written one and leave the latter uncancelled in the possession of the other party?

"'Dies Alba,' 'Rocks of Offense,' and 'Old Miasmas,' were published at different periods subsequent to the publication of 'City Lights.' They are all embraced in one contract, which bears date September 24, 1764. This contract is not at ten per cent. on the retail price, but at fifteen cents a volume on all volumes sold.

" This contract I claim to be invalid, because it was obtained from me under false representations, and because it is not equitable.

" Mr. Hunt asserts that before entering into this contract, and as a basis of this contract, he had a long conversation with me in which he fully

showed me the reason of the proposed change from
ten per cent. to fifteen cents on a volume. His
recollection of this conversation is so vivid that he
even recalls the sofa on which he sat. He thinks
he sent for me, but is not quite sure. He remembers that I was disposed at first to be trifling, but
he begged me to be serious, and assured me that
this was a serious matter. He remembers using
the expression, 'that their house was shaking in
the wind.' He says, he explained to me over and
over again the state of affairs and the reasons which
necessitated the change; and repeatedly asked me,
'Do you understand this clearly?' and I answered
that I did, and 'Do you agree to it?' and I said
yes. He is so positive in his assurance that he ex-
presses the wish that he could take his oath on it;
the referees ask him if, in that conversation, 'City
Lights' was included among the other books, and
he replies, 'distinctly.' Then, in face of my repeated written and verbal assertions to him that I
had no recollection of any such conversation, he
fixes his eyes upon me and says, with emphasis, 'I
think, M. N., you *must* remember this.'

"I have already stated to the referees that I had
no recollection of any such conversation or of any
verbal agreement. I was willing to attribute the
assertion to a mistaken impression on the part of
Mr. Hunt. Now, after his positive, persistent, and

circumstantial assertion, I go further. I deny his assertion in part and in whole, in every point and particular. I deny it not simply as a mistaken impression, but I deny it as a question of veracity between Mr. Hunt and myself.

"As I have said before, I cannot be called upon to prove a negative. The burden of proof lies on Mr. Hunt who asserts the positive. He admits that he has no correspondence to show it, but affirms that I admit it myself in one of my early letters by saying, 'I dare say' I did have such a conversation. The letter to which he refers is my second letter of inquiry, written before my faith in him had been shaken, and before the question of such a conversation had assumed any prominence or arrested my attention. I had asked him, as my letters show, why he wanted me to take less than ten per cent. He had replied, that we had talked it over and I agreed to less. I replied that I knew I agreed to it, for here were the contracts, but why did he wish me to make such contracts? My exact words were, 'I don't remember ever talking the things over with you, but I dare say I did — or rather you talked and I nodded, — as usual. And of course I agreed, for here are the contracts that say so. . . . . Don't you see the trouble lies back of the contracts. Why did you *wish* me to be having seven or eight per cent. when other people are getting ten?'

Here it is seen that in the very beginning, almost before any suspicion was aroused, and before my attention was at all fixed upon the importance of this conversation, I, first, carelessly but distinctly assert that I remember no such talk; second, I found my recognition of my assent not upon any remembered talk but upon the written contract; and third, I reiterate my questions concerning what lay back of the contract in entire unconsciousness that the talk had anything to do with it.

" So then, the only testimony which Mr. Hunt can produce of a verbal agreement which vitiates one contract and forms the basis of another, is a letter of mine in which I distinctly affirm that I don't remember anything about it! Mr. Hunt is welcome to all the sunshine he can find in *that* cucumber.

" Again, Mr. Hunt cannot fix the time when this explanatory conversation occurred and this verbal agreement was made; but it was the basis of a contract which was executed on the 24th September. It would naturally, therefore, be somewhere within speaking distance of that time. Now, in my statement of the case, made out on the 22d October, 1768, and put into the hands of my friend Mr. Dane a few days after, and read before the referees, I said, ' I think it must have been at the time this contract was made out — but I cannot be sure as to the time, — that Mr. Hunt told me that they were going to pay me a fixed sum, fifteen cents on a volume, instead of a percentage;' adopting this course with their authors, 'on account of fluctuations, general uncertainties, and so forth.' In the following January my vague recollections were confirmed by finding unexpectedly, and without seeking it or knowing that I had it, a letter from Mr. Hunt dated September 23, 1764, from which I make the following extract: 'The contract has been delayed for a sufficient cause.' [He then gives the cause of the delay, namely, Mr. Brummell's absence]. 'The percentage will read fifteen cents per copy, as the business times are fluctuating the prices of manufacture so there is no telling to-morrow, or for a new edition, what may be the expenses of publication. So we reckon your percentage in every and any event as fixed at fifteen cents per volume on all your books. If it should cost $1.50 to make the volumes you are sure of your author profit of fifteen cents. The price at retail may be $1.50, $2.00, or $3.00, as the high or low rates of paper, binding, etc., may be, but *you* are all right. This arrangement we make now with all our authors. . . . .

"'As I write, the contracts are reported ready, so I enclose them. Sign both, and send back the one marked with red X. You keep one and we the other.'

"I submit, that this extract, bearing date the day before the contract, has every sign of being fresh information. All the circumstances combine with my own distinct recollection, apart from them, to show that a new contract was made at my suggestion, not with any view whatever of changing the terms, but because I thought if a contract was necessary with one book, it was with another. I did not know that there had been or was to be any change from percentage to a fixed sum, until this letter told me. The retail price of the books had gone up to $1.50, so that ten per cent. and fifteen cents were the same. In this letter no allusion whatever is made to any previous conversation on the subject of the change from percentage to a fixed sum. Is it credible, I ask, that Mr. Hunt should have sent for me; should have assured me that this was a very serious matter; should have explained it all to me over and over again; should have repeatedly asked me if I understood it; should remember the conversation five years after, so vividly that the intensity of his convictions cannot find adequate expression in simple declaration but craves the relief of an oath; is it credible, that in his letter of the period he should have made no allusion to this conversation, but should have mentioned the arrangement as then communicated to me for the first time, — as it actually was?

" But further than this, my diary for 1764, carefully kept, with not a day missing, shows that during the whole summer and autumn preceding the 23d September, 1764, I was not once in Athens ! "

[And yet again, — I set on foot an inquiry at the time but did not get an answer in season to use it before the reference, — Mr. Hunt distinctly remembered that he sat on a certain sofa in the new shop during the conversation which was the basis of the contract of September, 1764. But the firm did not move into the new shop till May, 1765 !

Now if Mr. Hunt should gratify himself with the wished-for oath, I am sure that the accusing angel who flies up to Heaven's chancery with it, will blush as he gives it in, and the recording angel as he writes it down, will drop a tear upon the word and blot it out forever.]

" But it may be urged, giving up the conversation and relying only on the letter, that in any event I accepted and assented to the new contract with a full understanding of its meaning and effect, and am hence bound by it. This I deny. The law always scrutinizes transactions between parties in confidential relations, as father and son, guardian and ward, attorney and client, husband and wife, and demands the utmost frankness and fullest disclosure of circumstances, allows no concealments,

and sets aside all contracts where any advantage is
gained by reason of the confidence reposed. It
recognizes the influence of superior position, and
the right to trust in the party occupying it, and demands the strictest honor on his part. I think my
position with my publishers comes within the scope
of this principle. In respect of the matters involved in this contract, were we or could we be
equal? They were practiced business men living
in the city, with full knowledge of all the details
of their affairs. It was their business to manage
the external material parts of books. I was living
in the country, with no knowledge of these affairs,
and as I supposed, no need and no means of acquiring it. It was my part to attend to the interior
and intangible souls of books. I could not look
into their business without neglecting my own; as
indeed I have been forced to do for sixteen months
past, and as I should do with equal pertinacity for
sixteen years, were it necessary. I never sent for
my accounts, except when I wanted money and
wished not to overdraw. When they came, I
scarcely did more than glance at the footing to
ascertain what was due me. Nor do I now see of
what use it would have been to examine them ever
so minutely. I was proceeding entirely on a basis of
confidence, which I think I had a clear right to assume, and which was complete and unimpaired

until the date mentioned in my first paper, when I awoke to the fact that I was not receiving what I seemed to be entitled to, and what, on the closest scrutiny, I believe to be my legal and equitable dues.

"Such being the relation of the parties, let us examine for a moment — that is a pulpit fiction, I mean for a good many moments — the inducements held out to me by my publishers, as they are found in this letter. I maintain that the proposed change from percentage to a fixed sum is so mentioned as directly — I do not say intentionally — to mislead me. It is held up as an arrangement peculiarly to my advantage, as guaranteeing me in any event against a loss to which I might otherwise be exposed, and as securing me my profits by some stronger· safeguard than I had before possessed. But whereas I was blind I now see that it guarantees me against no loss, and the only safeguard it presents, is a safeguard against any benefit which might accrue to me from the rise in prices. Mr. Hunt says, "if it should cost $1.50 to make the volumes, you are sure of your author profits of fifteen cents," — as if I should not have been just as sure of them had I received percentage! "The price at retail may be $1.50, $2.00, or $3.00, as the high or low rates of paper, binding, etc., may be, but *you* are all right," — whereas I was all wrong, for if I had kept to a percentage, and the retail price had become $3.00, I should have had thirty cents instead of fifteen.

" It was almost immediately after this contract that the retail price of all my books went up to $2.00, and has remained so ever since. This was a fact which my publishers had the means to foresee, but which I could not and did not anticipate or even conjecture. The absolute identity of ten per cent. and a fixed sum at the time of the new contract, together with their representations of its superior advantage to me, and my confidence in them, all combined to deceive me. I should have adopted the same reasoning and drawn the same inference if a year earlier I had been asked to change the ten per cent. to twelve and a half cents, which at that time amounted to precisely the same thing.

" Had I been distinctly told that my books were largely to advance in price, but that all the profit of the advance was to accrue to the publishers and none of it to me, should I have consented to such an arrangement? The referees and my publishers, in discussing these matters, plunged into an abyss of figures into which I cannot attempt to follow them. I do not even understand the jargon — I trust they will pardon the term — in which they appeared to be communicating ideas. I had provided

myself with a friend who was, I believed, fully competent to dive as deep as the best of them. But I
was not allowed to retain him, and I could only sit
in despair on the brink of the gulf and stare at the
spectacle. From the few intelligible sounds that
did reach me I infer that the sacrifices of publishers
in behalf of authors have never been fully appre-
ciated. I felt that in claiming ten per cent. I was
guilty of an extortion second only to that of David
Copperfield in suggesting to Mr. Dolloby eighteen
pence as the price of ' this here little weskit.' ' I
should rob my family,' says Mr. Dolloby, ' if I was to
offer ninepence for it.' It is gratifying to recollect
that the last winter was a mild one, so that the
cases of extreme suffering must have been rare. If
it were not for an occasional glimpse at our impertinent income-returns one would be inconsolable.
As it is, would the referees count it as bringing in
new facts if I should send one or two postage-
stamps to the retired clergyman whose sands of life
have nearly run out, and beg a receipt for returning
an income of fifty thousand dollars on a bi-annual
cash profit of three hundred dollars?

"But though I cannot bring up a fact from the
bottom of the sea, I can see a fact when it stares
me in the face on land. If there was any reason
except uncovenanted mercies for advancing my
copyright from twelve and a half cents to fifteen,

when the books went from $1.25 to $1.50, it must
have applied with equal force to advancing my
copyright from fifteen to twenty cents when the
books advanced from $1.50 to $2.00. I deny that
the increased cost of doing business should be reckoned solely on the side of the publisher as the justification of *his* receipts and profits, while the author
should be held down to the same fixed sum. The
same causes that increased the cost of doing business to Messrs. Brummell & Hunt as publishers,
increased in quite as large a ratio the cost of my
doing business as an author. Every conceivable
form of expenditure to which I was subjected was
all the time increasing, and I was as much in need
of a *pro rata* increase of receipts from my books as
the publishers could be. But Messrs. Brummell &
Hunt take the opposite ground and maintain that
no matter what the added expenditure of the author
may necessarily become, only a fixed sum shall be
allowed to meet it, while the vast increase of receipts and of profits shall be absorbed by the publisher alone. If this be justice, equity, or law, I
think we would better stop hammering on the jubilee house, and begin back again at the Ten Commandments.[1]

[1] The "jubilee house" seems to be a reference to the institution of
the jubilee year among the Hebrews, — a year in which impoverished
families might redeem the property from which, at any time during
fifty years previous, they had been forced to part. Thus we are told

"But though I was not able to follow my publishers through the technics and tactics of their business, there were two ways in which I might have formed and presented some opinion of the justice of their course. Had I been allowed, I would have called in other publishers and have asked them what would be a fair price for books with the character, dress, and sales of mine. I do not see that there could be any unfairness in this. They surely would not be likely to decide unjustly against their own craft, and they surely would be able to give an intelligent answer.

"From the inquiries which Mr. Dane has made among other publishers, I believe that the sum which Messrs. Brummell & Hunt allege that they have made on all my books represents much more nearly the profits which they made on a single one of them, 'City Lights,' and that the profits which accrued to themselves from the rise in the prices of books are much larger than they represent them.

"It was for the purpose of elucidating this matter, also, that the questions were sent to Messrs. Hunt, Parry, & Co. some days before the reference be-

that if a man purchased of the Levites, the house that was sold should go out in the year of jubilee. Such a house might long be known in the neighborhood as the "jubilee house." The hammering spoken of was probably connected with the repairing of some such lately redeemed house, and seems to point to an Eastern origin and locality for this narrative. — NOTE BY EDITOR.

gan. Had I known the profits of their firm, the number and sales of their books, and the profits of their periodicals, I should have been in a position to judge of the correctness of their statements regarding the cost and profits of my books. Mr. Parry objects to such testimony, as he says they may make a great deal of money in outside ways, by speculating in butter, for instance. Precisely. But they advertise themselves as a publishing house solely, not as a publishing and butter house. It is Hunt, Parry, & Co., publishers, not publishers and dairymen. When I am charged in my books with the cost of store-rent, I wish to know whether the rent is for packing-cases or butter-tubs. I am charged for insurance and clerk-hire. How can I tell whether the insurance and clerk-hire cover my share alone or whether they may not also embrace the safety and the management of the " Adriatic ? " There is a separate item for the cost of advertising; but I am told that in a single year the receipts of the firm for advertising in their periodicals are ten thousand dollars more than the cost to them of all the advertisements which they publish elsewhere. Undoubtedly the sagacity of the firm in managing their periodicals has much to do with that circulation which makes them so valuable as advertising mediums ; but is it not just possible that the quality of the writing has some slight influence on their circulation. Yet not only are the authors of the books and of the magazine articles often one and the same, but the articles themselves are frequently but extracts from the books, and the books themselves are frequently made up in part or in whole from the articles. I do not mention this as an advantage to the publishers and a disadvantage to the author, but simply to show that the book business and the magazine business are so interwoven that an investigation of the one, to be exhaustive, must be, to some extent, an investigation of the other. Messrs. Hunt, Parry, & Co. must give us all the data if we are to make their 'sums prove,' as the children say. As they decline to do this, and as I never learned to 'cipher in turkey rule,' they have everything their own way in arithmetic.

"Another point in Mr. Hunt's letter of explanation was, as he says, ' This arrangement we make now with all our authors.'

" When I wrote to Mr. Hunt about the last of August, 1768, that, contrary to what I had understood his assertion to be, several authors had ten per cent., and therefore I thought I ought to have ten per cent., the firm did not deny my premise, but simply said, ' In your letter you assume that we have but one set of terms with the various authors whose works we publish. In this you are in error. What we pay to any individual author is a matter quite between him, or her, and ourselves, and it is not our custom to make one author the criterion for another. Many elements enter into the case that would make a uniform rate impracticable. Independently of other considerations, the varying cost of manufacture caused by different styles of publication would alone preclude such an arrangement. We must therefore decline to admit such an argument into the case.'

" The fact is, it was not necessary to admit it, since it was already there — placed there by Mr. Hunt's own hands. It was offered as an inducement for me to accept the new terms, " this arrangement we now make with all our authors." Either, then, Messrs. Brummell & Hunt do make a uniform arrangement with all their authors or they do not. If they do, this last letter cannot be a correct statement of facts, and the question arises, what is that uniform arrangement ? If they do not, then Mr. Hunt's letter of September 23, 1764, cannot be true, and the representation which he held out to me of a uniform mode of payment as an inducement for me to come into the arrangement, was not a correct representation. To ascertain whether or not they did make such an arrangement, I applied to such authors as were within reach to know what were and had been their rates of payment. A. writes, 'I have always received a percentage.

I remember no change in 1764, unless that B. & H. about that time (perhaps earlier), without my asking it, raised the sum they paid me for a poem, by one third.' B. says, 'I have been content with ten per cent.' Messrs. Hunt, Parry, & Co. write to C., 'Even D. now has only ten per cent.' E. says, 'I never published but one book (prose) with Brummell & Hunt. . . . . I received on this the usual beggarly percentage.' F. says, 'Generally we go on the system of half profits. . . . . In regard to 'Old King Cole,' they print and sell and allow me a certain sum on each copy sold.' G. says, 'Brummell & Hunt have, I believe, allowed me ten per cent. on the retail price of my books.' II. says, 'I believe it (the book) was to have yielded ten per cent. if anything.' I. says, 'Messrs. H., P., & Co. have published four books for me. The three first sell for $1.25, and I receive twelve cents each copy. The last is a joint affair, published by subscription.' K. says, 'All my contracts have been for *one half the net profits.* The two volumes published by the Troubadours, were offered to Parry, but as he wanted to make other terms, I declined, and they went to the Troubadours. This is the sum of my transactions with Messrs. B. & H.'

"On Friday, April 16, Mr. Dane sent to Messrs. Hunt, Parry, & Co. certain questions, in writing,

which the referees now hold, asking them to cite
their contracts with other authors, and giving a list
of names. Did they meet this question fairly? On
Friday, April 23, they made their reply to my statement. On the question of contracts, they cited A.'s
collected poems, B.'s poems, F.'s 'Old King Cole,'
M.'s works (collected), a part of which had to be
bought from another publisher, and the works of
Theodore Winthrop, which I believe were not
asked for. All these they cited as examples of
works on which similar contracts to mine had been
made, and they cited no others. If these persons
had written no other works this would have been
fair as far as it goes. But these persons had written other works, and I maintain that Messrs. Hunt,
Parry, & Co. had selected out of these works those
that were most unlike mine in scope, style, cost,
and probable circulation, and said nothing whatever
about books by the same authors which would more
nearly resemble mine in these respects. A., besides his collected poems, his blue and gold and
cabinet editions of his poems, has written separate
poems and prose works, which have been issued in
separate editions, and which, therefore, furnish a
far more proper basis of comparison with mine.
But about these separate books they said nothing.
Of his separate books, a, b, c, d, e, they made no
mention. They brought up B. as one whose works

were treated in the same way as mine; but they
mentioned only his Poems, blue and gold, and his
Songs. They never hinted that he had printed
and they had published any prose book for him.
Yet it is these prose books, his novels and essays,
which form the true basis of comparison between
him and me. They cited F., but they cited only
his ' Old King Cole,' which they did not originally publish, and which they own by a peculiar
bargain, and said nothing about the original books
which they have published for him, novels, essays,
and stories. They cited M., but while bringing in his
collected poems, which were entangled in a bargain
with some previous contumacious publisher, one
Fussey, they said nothing of his separate volumes.
They cited Winthrop, but Winthrop, like Marley,
was dead to begin with ; and if the living have hard
work to hold their own against this enterprising
firm, what can be expected of the dead ?

" Here they rested their case so far as the contracts go ; but as a desire was expressed to see the
contracts, they promised to produce them next
morning. On Saturday, accordingly, we began
with one set of contracts which proved to be a
most perplexing medley — a sort of contra dance
between written contracts and verbal agreements
with the rattling of stereotype plates for tambour-
ines. As the government of Russia is said to be

despotism tempered by assassination, so the business
of Messrs. Hunt, Parry, & Co. may be said to be
conducted on the basis of written contracts annulled
by verbal agreements. If we were met for the
purpose of preparing a Mars Hill House Shorter
Catechism and should ask, ' What is the chief end
of a written contract?' Messrs. H., P., & Co.
would promptly reply, ' A written contract's chief
end is to be canceled by a verbal agreement and
annihilated forever!' According to their practice,
it seems that we all agree, in writing, as to what
we will do, for the sake of saying afterwards that
we won't do it.

"However, plodding my way along as best I
could through the contracts, with Mr. Markman's
kind assistance, I found, or thought I found, that for
one book its author received at first twenty per cent.,
he owning the stereotype plates. Whether this was
by written contract or verbal agreement Mr. Markman does not recollect. From 1762 to 1764, he re
ceived twenty cents a volume, the retail price, meanwhile, having advanced from one to two dollars.
Since then a written contract gives him twenty
cents a volume, the retail price being two dollars.

"A second book by the same author is on the
same principle, except that there is no written
contract.

"A third, in 1762, either by contract or verbal

agreement, was receiving twenty per cent. on $1.00, retail price, the author owning stereotype plates. In 1764 it was changed verbally from percentage to twenty cents a volume, the price having gone up to two dollars.

"While I was painfully thridding these labyrinthine ways, I was arrested by a proposition from some quarter that time should be saved by intrusting the further examination of these contracts to the referees. I had every confidence in the referees, but how could I make my argument concerning these contracts without having seen them ? It was said that I should be present and examine them with the referees; but the referees were about to disperse to the four quarters of the earth — or, as there are only two of them, I suppose it might be more strictly accurate to say, the two hemispheres — not to meet again till Thursday, when I was to make my final statement. Mr. Markman then said that he would have the principal points of the contracts copied and sent to me either Saturday afternoon or Monday; but on Tuesday I received a letter from him saying that his time has been so much occupied with matters relating to Mr. Hunt's absence, that he has not had time to complete the copyright memorandum which he promised to send me, but will surely send it to-morrow — all of which I do not in the least doubt, but it does not alter the fact that the information concerning the contracts, for which I asked ten days ago, has not yet been furnished ; that I am to hand in my argument on Wednesday, and find myself at home to write up the play of Hamlet with a pretty important part of Hamlet left out.

"From what goes in, however, I am left, like Providence among the heathen, not without witness. Accepting alleged verbal agreements, it seems that the author cited, in changing from percentage to a fixed sum, came down to a sum fixed as high as the highest of my percentage. That is, he, at his lowest, is precisely where I was at my highest. My sole ambition was to climb as high as the point where he stopped falling! Does this fairly make out the assertion, ' this arrangement we make now with all our authors ' ?

"But I cannot reason upon contracts which I have never seen. I fall back upon the statements made to me by the authors I have quoted, and on this ground I affirm that I have not fared as the other authors, even of Messrs. Hunt, Parry, & Co., have fared. Neither can I accept their allegations of verbal agreements which cancel written contracts. The only verbal agreement I know anything about is one that never existed. I did not intend to mention Mrs. ——— any further than I have done, but Mr. Parry has cited her case and I may therefore

be permitted to say that verbal agreements and explanations were brought to bear on her in the same
way. In a letter to me dated August 9, 1768, she
says, ' A letter arrived from Mr. Hunt [Thursday]
telling me that *he had explained as I knew*, just
what he had never once explained as he knew —
and I read it and denied totally all his assertions.'
August 20, 1768, she says, ' Do you see all the
contracts Mr. Hunt tells Mr. E. were verbal. I do
not believe Mr. ———— ever consented to change
to ten per cent., because he would have told me,
and besides you see he had fifteen per cent. for
the very last book he gave them ! . . . . And now
they say he made a verbal agreement with Mr.
Brummell who is dead and cannot say anything.
But they show no papers.'

" I have been a practitioner at law but four days,
and it becomes me to be modest; yet I will hazard
the remark, that a verbal agreement without witnesses, between two dead men, is as near nothing as
anything in the way of evidence can well be.

" Mr. Parry affirms that Mrs. ————'s sister
afterwards examined their books and found nothing
wrong therein, and that Mrs. ———— was subsequently satisfied. I saw Mrs. ———— in Paris on
her way to Asia, and it seemed to me that she
was very far from satisfied, but that she *was* worried out, and preferred peace to pence. One can

imagine Miss —— hunting up Messrs. Hunt, Parry, & Co.'s account books in pursuit of knowledge!

"Neither do I accept accounts as proofs of a verbal agreement. My accounts ran on for years, unchallenged, without any such agreement, though that agreement is now alleged as the basis of the accounts. J. wrote to me, May 11, 1768, 'In the accounts of sale I believe the price paid me was ten per cent. of the *original* retail price, that is, the "Ambrosia" was published at a dollar fifty and I have always received fifteen cents a copy on that. When paper became so high during the war, the price of the book was raised to $1.75, but I am pretty sure I never received seventeen and a half cents, but always only fifteen, yet, as the papers are at home, I cannot be certain; only in a little account of sale sent here this winter the reckoning was at fifteen cents a copy for one, and twelve and a half cents for the other, but the account covered a space of three years during which the books had been selling at $1.75 and $1.50 respectively; so that, literally, he has not been paying me ten per cent.; but I did not think much about it, taking it for granted that the extra price was due to hard times. But I do not know why our labor is the only labor to remain low-priced.' Here it will be seen that for three years J.'s accounts might have

been cited at any time as proof of a verbal agreement, though no such agreement had ever been
made or even alleged. Messrs. H., P., & Co. may
say that they have a right to infer that silence gives
consent, and that authors have no right to be so
loose in money matters. Leaving out any silence
which might arise from delicacy, I would say, it is
true that they ought to be more accurate and systematic, but surely we may say to our publishers,
as the crab remarked to his father, when rebuked
for going sidewise, ' Gladly, my father, would we
walk straight, if we could first see you setting the
example ! '

"But authors are not always to be blamed for
their silence. We are not very large buyers of our
own books and do not always know when the price is
raised. Surely we cannot be expected to sit inflexi-
bly upon our property, like Miss Betsy Trotwood,
watching the rates of sale. It was a considerable
time after L.'s story-book advanced in price before
its author discovered it; as soon as she did, she
made a note of it, and after a little trouble succeeded
in having her contract fulfilled. But any time
between the change and her discovery of it, her
account might have been alleged as proof of a verbal agreement which did not exist. I am, of course,
not saying that it would have been so, but that it
might have been so. What we want, therefore, is
facts, Mr. Gradgrind.

" Since writing this, Mr. Markman's memoranda
of contracts have put in an appearance, and if correct, show beyond question, that their letter of
September, 1768, was true, and that the statement
in Mr. Hunt's September 1764 letter was not true.
There is scarcely an approach to uniformity in the
arrangements made with authors. Taking those
books which most resemble mine, the contracts are
of every species. There are contracts for twenty
per cent. where the author owns the plates, and
ten per cent. where the publisher owns them.
Books that retail at $1.25 pay the author ten cents
per volume, or fifteen cents per volume, he owning
the stereotype plates, or twelve cents per volume,
or twelve and a half cents per volume ; books that
retail at $1.50 pay the author fifteen cents, and ten
cents ; books that retail at seventy-five cents pay five
per copy ; books that retail at $1.00 pay twenty cents
per copy ; books that retail at $2.00 and $1.75
do the same·; books that retail at $1.12 pay ten
cents. When a verbal agreement is alleged as a
substitute for a written contract, the substitute also
varies. Some of the contracts are for half profits.
I do not find a single example of a book that retails
at $2.00 and pays the author fifteen cents. I shall
depend upon the referees to discover any fault in
my figures, but I believe they are correct. When
a change is made from percentage to a fixed sum,

there is generally a decrease to the author, but not so great as in my case. The aggregate of one set of books at a percentage was $1.36¼; after the change to a fixed sum it amounted to $1.68. On some of the books there has been no change. So that when Mr. Hunt says, "this arrangement we make now with all our authors," whether he means that they change from percentage to a fixed sum, or whether he means that they make with all the same ratio of decrease that they make with me, he is equally incorrect. There is no sense in which his words can be understood, in which they are true."

[There is one sense in which they may be counted correct. If we construe them to mean, " We pay all our authors just as little as we think they will stand. You, being rather the most pliable of any, will bear the greatest reduction, and we have accordingly reduced you to the lowest point," they appear to be marvellously accurate.]

" I claim, therefore, that I never assented to the second contract because I never understood it, and because the representations made to me as inducements were not correct. I claim that Mr. Hunt's letter was calculated (I do not say intentionally) to mislead and deceive me ; that I was misled and deceived by it, and as the result of this deception, I signed a contract which deprived me of my plainest rights in the premises; and the accounts subsequently rendered were accepted by me in the same good faith with which I sought the contract, with scarcely an examination, certainly without the least suspicion.

" Of the books not named in the contracts I believe I need say little. Even had the second contract been valid, no understanding can be inferred from it as to the five books not included in it. Why should the second contract be taken as a guide any more than the first? The first was made under ordinary circumstances, the second under peculiar ones which soon changed. They did not themselves understand that the second contract governed all the rest, for they did not pay me fifteen cents but only ten cents on ' Holidays.' They say that it was a small book; but so was ' The Rights of Men.' Yet ' Holidays ' contained 141 pages, was retailed at $1.50, and paid me ten cents, while ' The Rights of Men ' contained 212 pages, retailed at $1.50, and paid me fifteen cents — no accounts being rendered till after the trouble began. Mr. Parry says that ' Holidays' was a different kind of book, a children's book with pictures, and therefore he supposed they did not class it with the others, but simply fixed a price which they thought equitable. But X.'s story-book was also a juvenile book, with pictures, of the same class as mine ; yet on that they paid by contract ten per cent. C.'s story-book was also an illustrated juvenile, and on that they paid half profits.

"But I hold that the contract pretending to cover 'Dies Alba,' 'Rocks of Offense,' and 'Old Miasmas,' is inoperative and void, and cannot regulate the compensation to which I am entitled by copyright on these three books; still less can it regulate the compensation to which I am entitled on subsequent ones. If a contract is void in the direct operation claimed for it, its inferential operation must be shadowy indeed. With all due respect, I hold that it is little less than absurd for Messrs. Hunt, Parry, & Co. to claim that I am bound to accept that contract as the basis of settlement for subsequent publications. I hold that on these five books, published under no contract, I may claim what is just according to the usages of the trade.

"I do not know what may be the result of the inquiries of the referees among publishers. Mr. Dane, as his letter shows, made careful investigations, and found no one who did not say that ten per cent. was the minimum price. I believe that no respectable publisher can be found in the country who, regarding the cost of the books and the number sold, will not say that ten per cent. on the retail price is the very lowest sum that an honorable

publisher would have paid me had the whole mat- •
ter been referred to his own honor.

"Nor is it necessary to scour the country for evidence, since Messrs. Hunt, Parry, & Co. recognize
such a usage themselves, even if they do not follow
it. On what other principle did they allow me ten
per cent. in the beginning on "City Lights," when
I was a new author, and they had the whole matter
of price in their own hands? During the reference
they have also offered to return to ten per cent.
Why should they offer ten per cent. in the beginning, and ten per cent. at the close, and skip about
meanwhile from six and two thirds to seven and a
half per cent. according to their fancy or caprice?
This is a specimen of piping on the part of publishers, and dancing on the part of authors, that I do
not propose to take part in.

"My claim to compensation on five hundred of
the fifteen hundred books exempted in the first edition of 'City Lights,' needs no labored argument.
Their attempt to prove from their books that I had
due notice of the fact, proves that I ought to have
had notice, while the accounts received and produced by me prove that no such notice was given me.
Mr. Markman thinks it may have been lost in the
mail, but the accounts which I hold cover the whole
time of my transactions with Messrs. Brummell &
Hunt, and I submit that the mails shall be believed

innocent till they are proved guilty, and that Messrs. Brummell & Hunt must be nipped in the bud, or they will soon, as Sidney Smith says, be speaking disrespectfully of the equator. Mr. Parry admits that without explanation the word edition means a thousand copies. He also admits that in all cases when more than a thousand copies are exempted, the specific number is given. He believes mine to be the only exception to this rule. He alleges as the reason of this unusual exemption the unusual cost of my books, saying that they cost a great deal more than any other on their list. To this I reply that I should have been told in the beginning that they did or would cost more than others. Mr. Markman then brings forward a letter of mine to prove that I *was* told, and did know that the books cost more. This letter bears date September 20th, 1762, two days after the publication of 'City Lights,' and the extract says: ' The fact that I wish to impress upon your mind is that you have tricked out my book so beautifully that nothing could be lovelier. You would not have done it though, if I had not threatened you within an inch of your life, would you? [etc., etc., etc.] But now see, I never thought till yesterday that they must cost more than the other way, and I have been distressed all along and this makes me more so,' etc.

" This does not prove what Mr. Markman introduced it to prove, but it proves just the opposite, which is the next best thing. It shows that until the day after the book was published I had never thought of the book's cost, and that then the thought was spontaneous, not suggested to me by others. It proves beyond question that nothing had ever been said to me about it.

" On one or two other points, not strictly necessary to the case but introduced by Mr. Parry, I must beg a moment's forbearance. Mr. Parry, feeling that my claim involves fraud, reads extracts from my early letters, to show that I was very urgent to publish ' City Lights,' that I expressed the greatest confidence in them, and that, in short, I came to them in such a way as, to use his own language, would have almost held out a temptation to defraud me. So that if they had been disposed to defraud me at all they would have done it then.

" Fraud is a hard word, and I believe I have not used it ; but if Mr. Parry insists, I will say that the exemption of the fifteen hundred books under cover of *an edition* occurred with the first edition of my first book, and I really don't see how they could have begun *much* earlier if they had tried.

" Mr. Parry mentions as a proof of their friendly intentions, that they desired to refer the whole matter to Mr. Rogers because they thought he was my friend ; that they offered to refer it to my friend

Mr. Brook, of whom they knew nothing, and to my friend Mr. Greatheart, of whom they knew very little. It will be observed that they did not once ask me to select a friend, but generously took the whole burden of the selection upon themselves.

"The first person to whom they offered to refer it was Mr. Rogers, and I accepted him gladly. I was so much in earnest that I wrote him myself begging him not to decline — and this although I had never seen him. On account of his health he felt obliged to decline ; but before he had declined, Messrs. Hunt, Parry, & Co. proposed to relinquish him, for what reason I do not know. They proposed that I should give up Mr. Russell, and they should give up Mr. Rogers, and we should each make a new selection. I was entirely satisfied both with my choice and theirs, and I saw no reason for changing. So that I not only accepted the nail they drove, but I clinched it myself. I not only kept to my own choice, but I had to make them keep to theirs. It was while they stood thus shivering on the brink, after Mr. Rogers had been proposed and accepted, and before he had declined, that they proposed Mr. Brook and Mr. Greatheart.

"But was it friendly in them to turn away from their own choice, and go about among my friends choosing persons of whose qualifications they were ignorant, forcing me to reject them, and thus to discriminate against my own friends? Did not Messrs. Hunt, Parry, & Co. know that this was a matter not to be settled by sentiment? I should have considered it a far more unequivocal sign of friendliness if they had permitted me to appear before the referees with the friend whom I had intelligently chosen, who had stood by me through the whole trouble, who was familiar with all the details of my case, and capable of understanding all the details of theirs, and by whose aid, therefore, arbitration might be satisfactory as well as conclusive. Instead of which they compelled me to stand alone, unaided, without preparation, without the possibility of being prepared, in a position for which their long acquaintance with me must have told them I was eminently unfit, and which one at least of their number must have known would be to me peculiarly embarrassing and distressing. Their idea of a friendly arbitration seems to be that of imposing upon me the friends I do not want, and taking away from me the friend I do want.

"Mr. Parry thinks indeed that Mr. Dane had poisoned my mind regarding them. But he also thought Mrs. ———'s mind was jaundiced. Perhaps that question belongs to the doctors rather than the referees. Whether it be poison or jaundice it is to be hoped the disease may not spread.

"There are other parts of Mr. Parry's statements

which I should like to lay before the referees, but I
remember that they are mortal, and though the
spirit is willing the flesh is weak, and I forbear.

" IN CONCLUSION,

I claim that my first contract for 'City Lights,'
specially stipulating ten per cent., shall be carried
out in good faith; and that it shall not be considered as changed or modified by any conversation
remembered by Mr. Hunt, but absolutely denied
by myself. And I claim that the word edition
used therein shall be held to mean just what Mr.
Parry admits it would mean in common accepta-
tion with the book-trade, namely, one thousand
copies.

"2. I claim that my second contract, covering
'Alba Dies,' 'Rocks of Offense,' and 'Old Miasmas,' was obtained from me under a total misapprehension of facts, that this misapprehension of
mine was the result of a misrepresentation (I do
not say intentional) made to me by Mr. Hunt in
his letter of September 23, 1764, wherein he represents the arrangement as one uniform among their
authors and as assuring me a rate of compensation,
which he leaves me to infer, I might not otherwise
obtain, whereas he knew that the arrangement was
not uniform and that my percentage would amount
to more as prices were then tending, — and the ar-

rangement was made by him so as to prevent my ten per cent. from amounting to more than fifteen cents per copy. This I did not understand, and should not have assented to if I had understood it. I hold that neither in law, equity, morals, nor manners should I be held to an agreement which I did not comprehend, which the opposite party so presented as to prevent my comprehending it, and which deprived me of my proportionate share of an increase of profit admitted to have been made on the books published under it. The contract, therefore, should be set aside, and I should be paid according to the usage of publishers, or at the same rate as appears in the contract for ' City Lights,' namely, ten per cent.

" 3. I claim that on my books published since the date of my second contract, and not alluded to or included in either contract, namely, ' Winter Work,' ' Holidays,' ' Pencillings,' ' Cotton Picking,' and ' Rights of Men,' my compensation shall be fixed by the usage existing among publishers and authors.

" 4. I claim and must certainly be entitled to receive interest at the rate of seven per cent. on all sums found to be due me at the date of the several semi-annual settlements, counting my compensation uniformly at the rate of ten per cent. on the retail price of the books at the date of the settlement. This point is so plain that it can need no argument.

"5. I claim that I am equitably entitled to damages to compensate me for the loss that has resulted to me pecuniarily and otherwise from this unhappy occurrence. My pecuniary damage alone amounts to more than three thousand dollars. There are hurts of other kinds to which money bears no relation.

"My actual expenses in preparing for this reference have been very considerable, and under the award of costs I claim that I should have an ample allowance made me to cover my outlays in this regard."

After this statement had been read, Messrs. Hunt, Parry, & Co. were permitted to make whatever of reply they chose. They denied no fact, and challenged no inference in my statement.

The referees, after two days of deliberation, returned the following decision:—

"The undersigned, mutually agreed upon as referees in the matter in controversy between M. N. and Messrs. Hunt, Parry, & Co., on their own account, and as successors of Brummell & Hunt, hereby award to M. N. the sum of twelve hundred and fifty dollars, to be paid her by Hunt, Parry, & Co., within three days from the date of this paper in full compensation for her claims upon the matter in this controversy — and that hereafter M. N. shall receive ten per cent. copyright on the retail price of all her books printed by Hunt, Parry, & Co., except the three books embraced in the contract between the parties dated September 24, 1764. The referees decline any compensation for services or expenses and leave each party to pay their own costs.

"Signed and delivered, April 30, 1769.

"J. RUSSELL.
"G. W. HAMPDEN."

X.

AVING trespassed so far on the patience of the reader, I may as well presume a little further, and indulge in a few reflections.

First, from the investigations and observations of the last two years, I infer that authors are very much to blame in their business dealings. By their inexactness, their indifference, their unreasonable and indolent trust, and their excessive monetary stupidity, they not only become an easy prey of, but they offer a direct temptation to the cupidity of publishers. Not a single author to whom I appealed showed the slightest reluctance to answer my questions, nor, I may almost add, the slightest ability to answer them adequately. For instance, the points I wished to ascertain were whether a writer was paid by percentage or by a fixed sum : what was the percentage and what the fixed sum : and whether during or subsequent to the year 1764 any change was made in the mode or rate of payment.

See now how charmingly the authors met my points.

Says one, " Brummell and Hunt never published but —— with me and I received on this the usual beggarly percentage ; " leaving me entirely in the dark as to what was the beggarly percentage.

Says another: " What terms do I make with B. & H. ? Yes, with all my heart. In regard to ——, they print and sell and allow me a certain sum on all copies sold ; " but with the greatest inclination in the world giving me no hint of the amount of that " certain sum."

Says another : " Brummell & Hunt have, I believe, allowed me ten per cent. on the retail price of my books. That was the first arrangement at least, but I must confess I never look at their statements of account."

Says a fourth : " I have always received a percentage. . . . . I remember no change in 1764, unless that B. & H. about that time (perhaps earlier) without my asking it, raised the sum they paid me for ——, etc. . . . . The interests of authors and publishers are identical — a fact which they understand better than we do."

Yet the firm testified of this very writer that they had written agreements to pay him percentage, and that when prices advanced they waived the percentage, and paid him a certain (lower) sum per volume.

A fifth says: " I have not the least objection in the world in replying to your letter in the most straightforward way. . . . . I have been contented with ten per cent. on the retail price of my printed books."

Yet the written contracts of this writer showed every variety of arrangement from twenty per cent. downward.

A sixth says: " Messrs. B. & H. have published four books for me. . . . . The three first named sell for $1.25, and I receive twelve cents each copy."

But Messrs. B. & H. affirmed that these books sold for $1.50 each.

A seventh says: " I did not send your letter to ——, for the reason that she does not know as much as you do about the subject of its inquiry. The most she could tell you would be, that now and then there comes a bit of paper very neatly and tastefully diversified by red and blue lines, and dreadfully complicated by sundry hieroglyphics, which she has been told are figures, and that a check embellished with one of the rows of figures accompanies it. . . . . I have an impression that years ago, when —— was taking such sesquipedalian strides to public favor, Mr. Brummell told me that after the number of copies sold had reached a certain point, the author received a reduced percentage, and I think I remember wondering by what perversion of commercial philosophy, an article of which fifty thousand copies could be sold, was worth less, proportionally, than one of which only five thousand could be bartered, for of course the ratio of cost decreased with every successive thousand manufactured."

Here, it will be perceived, is a faint glimmer of sense, which will be completely extinguished by the next extract.

"—— said you made a mistake in thinking yourself differently used from the rest of the writing craft, and explained that the profits of the author did not keep up the same proportion in repeated editions, but went to pay the increased circulation. For his part he would rather be more poorly paid for the sake of being more widely read."

Must not that have been an explanation worth having? It is not difficult to conjecture the source whence that form of explanation originated, for another letter says, " Mr. —— went to see Mr. Hunt. . . . . Mr. Hunt expressed great regret that it had all happened ; said ' Rights of Men,' had done more for your reputation than any other book ; that you made more than the publishers did, etc., and that they thought better to have a low per cent. and large sales, than the contrary ; though I don't see what a low per cent. paid to the author has to do with large sales, if the price of the book is kept high to purchasers."

The fact, is that as a bad woman is said to be a great deal worse than a bad man, so a man innocent of business capacity, is far more innocent than any woman can be. A woman may be never so silly, but there is generally a substratum of hard sense somewhere. A man may be never so wise, and yet completely destitute of this practical ability. It is largely in behalf of these helpless, harmless, deluded, and betrayed gentlemen, that I have felt called to take up arms. What sword would not leap from its scabbard to maintain the cause of the weak and the wronged?

But though I admit and lament that authors are unpractical and unbusiness-like to the last degree, I must affirm that they have less inducement to be business-like and less opportunity to be practical than any other class of persons. Suppose a writer sets out with the determination to be prudent and sagacious, where shall he begin? If a farmer has a bushel of potatoes to sell, he knows, or can learn in a moment, precisely their market value. The Early Rose has its price, and the Jackson White has its price; there is no room for doubt, or misgiving, or mistake. But the author has not and cannot have the least notion of the market value of his products. He does not even know their intrinsic value. He does not know whether he has raised an Early Rose or a dead-and-gone Chenango. He may have spent his strength on what is absolutely unsalable. His work is production, but for its worth he must depend solely on the word of those who buy and sell. After a while he does indeed arrive at something like a scale of value, but he never reaches such a degree of certainty as to feel assured of any special piece of work. Every one must be judged by itself. Five successful books are no absolute guaranty that the sixth will not be worthless.

It seems to me, also, that there is no business in which so few checks exist as in that of publishing. An author, we will say, agrees to receive ten per cent. on the retail price of all copies of his works that are sold, but he has literally nothing but the publisher's word by which to know how many copies are sold. The manufacturer knows how many he has made, but it would be offensive to ask for the manufacturer's accounts, and moreover he would probably not render them if asked. He would consider it as betraying the secrets of the trade, or the trust of his employers, or otherwise impertinent and unwarranted. Of course a false return of sales would be fraud, and somewhat complicated fraud; but human ingenuity combined with human depravity has been known to surmount obstacles to crime as formidable as these; and the danger of detection is infinitessimally small. If there be any such thing in arithmetic as the Double Rule of Three, — and

I seem to have a vague impression that there is, — it may well be brought to the solution of the problem : if a publisher may for years safely disregard, not to say violate, the condition of a contract which an author has before his eyes in plain black and white, how long may another publisher safely falsify accounts which an author never sees, and which he could not understand if he should see ? I have no doubt that in nine cases out of ten, and perhaps also in the tenth, the returns of sales are as accurate as the moral law. What I maintain is, that the author, be he wise as Solomon, has no means of knowing whether they are or not, while the manufacturer of all other goods knows precisely how much raw material goes into the mill and how much of the manufactured article comes out.

If the author, instead of receiving a percentage, takes half profits, he is even more at the mercy of the publisher. In the very outset the wildest theories prevail as to what constitute profits, and though the author may make heroic struggles to be exhaustively mathematical, the probabilities are that the only draught made upon his science will be the very simple effort of dividing by two whatever sum the publisher has chosen to figure up. The plan adopted by actors and actresses, to take half the gross receipts, is far more simple and sensible.

It is true that an author may take advantage of

competition and seek a second market if the first prove unsatisfactory, but it is also certain that he cannot do this to any effective extent without serious injury to himself. All the skill, the vitality, the invention, the thought, which he brings to the disposition of his wares is so much taken from his producing power. He ought to be wholly free to do his best work. He ought to be able to concentrate himself on his writing. If he must turn aside to study the state of the market and superintend the details of sale and circulation, that necessity will surely tell in the deterioration of his works; and even at that cost he will not be so good a business manager as one who is to the manner born. It is a very pretty thing to be a poet-publisher — in the newspapers, but if the poet's imagination happens to get loose among the publisher's facts, it makes sad work, and it is not merry work when the publisher crops out in the poet's verses.

What then remains? It has been proposed that authors combine and form a publishing-house by themselves, publishing their own books and receiving their own profits. This plan looks simple enough, but I must confess it seems to me chimerical in the last degree. Excepting the temptations of their trade, doubtless a hundred publishers are as honest as a hundred authors, and surely they have a great deal more business sagacity.

But as soon as authors turn publishers they fall into all the publisher's temptations without acquiring his business power; so that when you have chemically combined author and publisher you have an amalgam wholly and disastrously different from either of the original simples, namely, a publisher minus his common sense.

No, the publisher is not an artificial member of society. Like all other middle-men he meets a real want. He exists because in the long run it is cheaper and better for writers to employ him than to do his work themselves. Of course, the wiser and more righteous he is, the better he answers the end of his creation; but with all his imperfections on his head, he is better than nobody. A man may as well undertake to build his house with his own hands to save himself from the short-comings and extortions of carpenters, as to manufacture and distribute his own books to save himself from the extortions of publishers. We may send missionaries among them, we may gather them in to our Sunday-schools, but we need not think to exterminate them.

Authors may form publishing houses, and those houses may be successful, but if so it will be simply by adopting substantially the methods of successful publishing-houses already established. It seems to me easier and more economical to let such

17

institutions spring from the soil, rather than attempt to construct them out of material which has already been organized into another form of life.

Shall we then take the publishers *cum grano salis*, and try to guard our interests by keeping a strict look-out? We must turn publishers ourselves to make it of any account. A detective, to be worth anything, ought to be at least as wily as the rogue he watches, and to be so he must give his mind to it, and if he give his mind to that, wherewithal shall he set up any other business? An author need not rush in among publishers as Cincinnati swine are said to invade the streets with whetted knives, crying " come and eat me"; but if he on the contrary objects, steadfastly and stoutly, to being devoured, he does not know where his vulnerable point is, and cannot therefore arm himself against attack. He is not and cannot become, consistently with the proper pursuit of his own profession, sufficiently acquainted with the details of publishing to know whether a measure proposed by a publisher be or be not fair. For instance, the publisher contracts to pay ten per cent. on the retail price of a sixty-two cent book. A war comes, bringing high prices, and the book goes up to a dollar and a quarter. The publisher continues to pay the author ten per cent. of sixty-two cents, making no reference to the increased price. The author presently chances to discover it, and remonstrates. The publishers say curtly, "You will make the price of the book so large that it will have no sale," oblivious of the fact that it is not the author but themselves who have raised the price of the book. He replies that the price is not his affair ; he must insist upon the contract. The publishers yield, and the author is apparently victorious. But when a second author brings up this case as a reason why he should receive his percentage, the publishers reply, " True, we did continue percentage because he insisted, but, as a warning, the book had a very poor sale." But what effect on the sale can the author's twelve and a half, instead of six and a half cents have if the price to the buyer is the same ? Until some better answer is given I shall believe that the sale diminishes because the publisher chooses it ; because he prefers to sacrifice a small sum on a single volume as a warning to contumacious authors, rather than encourage rebellion by continuing to receive profits of which he must divert a larger share to the author. If he can, by one or two examples, show restive writers that the question is not between six and a half cents and twelve and a half cents on a thousand books, but between six and a half on a thousand, and twelve and a half on a hundred, the sum he sacrifices in showing it is not a bad investment.

Since, then, the publisher has matters within his own grasp so entirely that what he is forced to pay with one hand he can easily pluck with the other, I do not clearly see the advantage to be gained by insisting on any special bargain with him. Perhaps I do not quite know what I am talking about. I suspect, on the whole, I do not. But my remarks are all the more valuable for that. If, after two years of clapper-clawing among a quartette of cats, a mouse is still unskilled in feline ways, in what state of helplessness must be those unadventurous little things who have never left their holes?

But there are the books of the firm which the suspected publisher opens to you with a frankness of innocence that ought to disarm and convince the most hardened unbeliever. Any demur is met by an invitation to come and look at "the books." The trail of the Serpent is over all the rest of the world, but "the books" have escaped the contamination of original sin and shine with the purity of Paradise. Burglars blow open safes, banks and directors and cashiers and tellers come to grief, but "the books" always tell the truth, the whole truth, and nothing but the truth. Nowithstanding which I, from the beginning, instinctively gave those "books" a wide berth. They were to me like the "magick bookes" of Spenser's hermite. "Let none them read." That "the books" are not always " reliable gentlemen " will have been inferred from the account which they professed to have sent me, and which was — lost in the mail. That " the books " are not always intelligible witnesses would appear, could we know how many unwary persons have gone to them in pursuit of knowledge, and found the difficulty insurmountable. " We had the books here," said one benighted author of no mean repute, " and I examined them, and Kate examined them, and Frank examined them, and the Major examined them, and we could make nothing of them." That the books have been made to do yeoman's service in this battle has already been seen, and by various tokens it would seem that they have not yet been dismissed the service. Only to-day a letter says, " But the account of the sales of your book and the sums paid you for them, as I derived them from the books of Mr. Hunt, convinced me that whatever the bargain might be you had a better one than *I* had. I have half profits — you have had more."

That is what " the books" say unquestionably ; but what a stiff-necked and perverse author refuses to believe without further proof. When a publisher shows me receipted bills for the sums he has actually paid in manufacturing and publishing my books, and for the sums he has received from their sale, I will — take them to an expert for examination ; but when he proposes to set me down before a mighty maze of figures, which for aught that appears, may all have been conjured up by his imagination, and begs me to deduce from them any conclusion whatever, I decline with thanks. That contention I leave off before it be meddled with. It is not necessary to be a Solomon in order to know enough to keep away from figures which it is necessary to be a Solomon to understand, and which when understood are much like the "litle flyes cal'd out of deepe darknes dredd" by the hermite before referred to, and which, —

> "Fluttring about his ever-damned hedd,
> Awaite whereto their service he applyes,
> To aide his friendes, or fray his enemies."

There remains also to the wronged or suspicious author recourse to the law or to the more informal arbitration, but this also is vanity. To me a lawsuit seemed utterly intolerable, but my experience of arbitration was so repulsive, and is so hideous in memory — and this solely from the nature of things, since, alike from the referees and from Messrs. Parry and Markman who, like St. Paul, were the chief speakers, on the other side, I met only courtesy — that a lawsuit seems attractive in comparison; but if I had instituted a lawsuit, without doubt adverse fate hereafter would have been implored to take any shape but that! If two parties are really bent on getting at the vital facts, presenting absolute truth, securing exact and essential justice, nothing can be more to the purpose apparently than a reference to disinterested, non-professional, intelligent, and friendly persons; but two parties honestly bent on such an object would probably have nothing to quarrel over. Even if they have it is not certain that the informal is better than the formal mode of settlement. If there are no facts to be hushed up, a legal investigation will do no harm ; if there are facts to be hushed up, a legal investigation is necessary. We look at the law as at best a clumsy round-about way of arriving at just conclusions — a method full of ingenious devices to entangle and confuse witnesses and make the worse appear the better reason. We take the informal arbitration as a short cut to the desired goal. On the whole I am inclined to think that the law is the shortest cut in the known world. The rules which obtain in courts of justice and which seem to the unprofessional mind a mere medley of arbitrary vexations and restrictions, are the result of the experience of ages, and with all their short-comings and their long-comings do probably present the most expeditious and unerring mode of reaching truth which human wit and wisdom have yet devised. If so we cannot depart from them without loss. In ridding ourselves of their clumsiness we rid ourselves also of their effectiveness. We rend away the red tape, but the package immediately falls apart into a worthless heap, of memoranda. You avoid a lawsuit because of the publicity and multiplicity and infelicity of lawyers, witnesses, judge, and jury. You adopt a reference because it dispenses with all these and goes straight at the heart of things. But you find by experience that unless your opponent wishes it you may not get at the heart of things at all. In a lawsuit you can enforce measures; in a reference you are dependent upon courtesy. Your opponent presents only that which is good in his own eyes. He produces what he chooses; he withholds what he chooses. To be sure you do the same; but you, angel that you are, have nothing to hide, while he, the fiend! has all manner of wiles and wickedness to conceal. If now you were in court, politeness and impertinence would be equally and wholly out of the question. It is the duty and delight of lawyers to find out everything — and such is the depravity of the legal heart, it is especially their duty and delight to ferret out what the opposite party desires to conceal. It is not what a man wishes and means to say, but everything which he can be made to say, that a lawyer wants. His hand can put aside the proffered " books," and grab the books which are withheld.

He does not permit the opposite parties to select and exclude witnesses, but goes out into the highways and hedges and compels to come in whom he wants. The law winds a long way round, but it sets you down as near your journey's end as the nature of things permits. A private reference takes a short cut, but it has no inherent power to carry you far from your starting-point. Arbitration has the advantage in respect of privacy, and that is an advantage not to be overestimated. Still, if there is anything to choose when both are intolerable, it seems rather worse to speak yourself before five men, than to have some one else to speak for you before five hundred. It matters not how wise, how impartial, referees may be, their jurisdiction is necessarily limited, and they cannot go beyond it to compel, or extort, or present. They must judge on what is spontaneously set before them. If to avoid trouble and unpleasantness be your object, it is better to submit to everything and keep out of strife altogether. If you set out to accomplish an end, it is better to shut eyes and ears to disagreements, and take the road which common experience designates as the surest and safest in the long run.

But I most heartily advise writers in general to do neither. So far as the improvement of one's fortune goes, nothing is more futile. One should be exact, prompt, methodical, and intelligent so far as possible. He will thus exert a salutary influence over his publisher, and will be far more likely to receive his dues than if he believes " in uninquiring trust " and lives wholly by faith. But it is better for his purse to take what a publisher chooses to give than to make an ado about it afterwards. Even if successful in regard to the particular sum he claims, it is at a cost of time and trouble altogether disproportionate to it. He plays an unequal game at best, because the publisher's business goes on serenely, during all the difficulty, while the author's must be at a stand-still. The very instrument that he uses in defending his works is the instrument which he ought to be using in producing them. Even as a pecuniary transaction it is far more profitable to sow seed for future harvests than to spend strength in trying to secure the gleanings of last year's growths. The money proceeds of the insurrection, whose history has been given in these pages, was twelve hundred and fifty dollars. The whole amount claimed to make up ten per cent. was about three thousand dollars, and considering that my whole plan of proceedings was demolished in the beginning, and that the case had to present itself, as one may say, smothered in a mass of irrelevant details, and deprived of much that was to the purpose, I reckoned myself extremely well off. But even had the whole sum been awarded, it would have been no very munificent compensation for eighteen months of literary labor, apart from the fact that the labor was of a kind for which no money could compensate. In its baldest shape, the results of a year and a half of work were twelve hundred and fifty dollars, or little more than one third of what was claimed on previous work. I think myself therefore justified in asserting that though quarreling with your publishers may be very good as a crusade, it is a very poor way of getting a living.

Let me here correct an impression that seems to prevail somewhat extensively as to the rewards of literary life. It certainly has its rewards, and of the most delightful kind. What joys it may bring in the higher walks I do not know, but even on the lower levels, I should like to live forever — a thousand years to begin with, at any rate. I could speak as enthusiastically as a certain popular writer, " once more famous than now," " Of all the blessings which my books have brought me, — blessings of inward wealth that cannot be so much as named, — blessings so rich, so divine, that I sometimes think nothing ever was so beautiful as to have written a book."

But so far as literature pays cash down it is not

to be compared to — shoemaking, for instance. The daily papers have been circulating a paragraph to the effect that a recent popular book had gone to a second edition and that its author had already received from it twelve thousand dollars. I am not prepared to deny the statement; but I know an author of nine books, not it is to be hoped on the same footing of intrinsic merit, but books which have travelled up to nine, ten, and fourteen editions, whose author never has received and never expects to receive twelve thousand dollars on the whole lot.

Let nothing in this remark be construed into anything like complaint. On the contrary, authors ought to be grateful to their publishers for allowing them so large a gratuity. As Mr. Parry remarked concerning the appropriation of an edition of fifteen hundred books to the use of the firm, they might have taken more if they had chosen. And when we reflect that not only do they bestow upon us these large sums of money, but, as sundry extracts in other parts of this volume show, they first manufacture for us the fame which brings the money, we are, in the language of the hymn, lost in wonder, love, and praise. It must be heart-rending to fashion your graven image and then have that image turn upon you and demand a share of the profits !

Unhappily a dense ignorance upon this subject broods over the community, and there should be added to our literature an

AUTHOR'S CATECHISM.

1. *Question.* Can you tell me, child, who made you?

Answer. The great House of Hunt, Parry, & Co., which made heaven and earth.

In controversies with publishers, the author is at a signal disadvantage by reason of the connection of publishers with the press. Publishers have the entrée of the newspapers by their advertising, and all in the way of business, it is the easiest thing in the world to give public opinion a tilt in the desired direction without the least suspicion on the part of the reader, or any more collusion on the part of the editor than is implied in a good-natured relinquishment of a few lines of editorial space. Here, we will say, is a house which advertises to the extent of hundreds, perhaps thousands of dollars in a single paper. In connection with an extraordinary advertisement, it hands to the editor an extraordinary paragraph, celebrating its more extraordinary virtues. The advertisement goes in among the advertisements, and the eulogy goes in among the editorials and becomes the voice of the paper.

Nobody is hurt, and the firm is greatly helped in building up for itself name and fame. When the Athenian newspapers glow with reflections upon the inability of authors to understand the details of publishing and the unimpeached and unimpeachable honor of the house of Hunt, Parry, & Co., not half a dozen readers suspect that those reflections are anything but the spontaneous tribute of a grateful people to the eminent firm in question. Nobody suspects that behind all the glitter and glory some pestiferous little author is poking an inquisitive finger in among those details, is indeed questioning that unimpeached and unimpeachable honor, and that this beating of gongs is but Chinese strategy on the part of the attacked to scare away the impertinent foe. I can make no avowal on this head, having nothing but internal evidence to go upon: but applying the rules of Scriptural exegesis, it seems to me that we attribute to the four Gospels a divine origin on less evidence than we may attribute to these eulogies a common origin.

For instance, during that portion of the sidereal year known throughout the solar system as Jubilee week, the press of Athens burned with enthusiasm for the house of Hunt, Parry, & Co.

"The broadside advertisement," says one, "with which the renowned publishing house of Messrs.

Hunt, Parry, & Co. salute the country in this jubilee time on another page of this morning's Post, will excite universal attention and remark. It details the literary achievements of this enterprising firm during the last year and a half in a form that is both novel and impressive. Where are the publishers on this continent who within that term have presented to the reading public works from [how many?] different authors, nearly all of whom are living celebrities? It would be glory enough for any firm to have announced original works from less than one fourth that number of well-known authors. Read the glittering roll of names as they are presented. In poetry, L., T., L., B., and W. Of novelists, D., T., S., H., H., R., and G. And of essayists, travellers, writers on natural history and science, such a shining company of men and women of genius as will make book-shelves brilliant for all time to come. But these publishers have not compromised quality with quantity. They hold up to their high standard in every essay in which they engage. Nor are they in any sense such devotees of Mammon as to think it possible to build a lasting reputation on anything less substantial than true honor in dealing as well as indisputable worth in selection.

" Their shelves and counters are an embarrassment of literary riches. Such a display of the ripest fruits of culture, taste, judgment, enterprise, and business sagacity cannot be surpassed. Their wonderful march to their eminent and leading position as publishers has given an excellent example to the country in refining and solidifying the common rules of business in their own field, and elevating and dignifying a branch of trade than which not one is clothed with nobler and purer associations. From this house, also, go forth a quarterly, two monthlies, and a weekly magazine, any one of which would add lustre to the repute of the publishers. None but sound and sweet literature comes from hence. It is the aim of the firm to keep the fountain clear from which such incessant streams of influence are to flow. American authors contribute in large store to the rich treasury of its productions, while foreign, and especially British writers supply in large degree the stores of reading, which are the recreation and delight of cultivated people everywhere."

And thus another paper takes up the parable : —

" Our first page to-day is entirely devoted to a remarkable advertisement, which tells the story of rare business enterprise, and is filled to overflowing with attractive announcements. But it is for characteristics other than these that it will command attention and really deserve study. Within a year and a half, Hunt, Parry, & Co. have given to the public works from the pens of two score of authors, American and English, almost all of them living and of widest popularity. To represent in print a half-dozen of the most prominent on the list might be the making of any firm; to take care of the whole of them would seem to be an embarrassment of riches. But the establishment has done and is doing this, with unremitting energy and in good style. We need not take room to run over the long and brilliant catalogue; a glance at the eight columns will reveal a galaxy of shining names. Observe the poets, — T., B., L., and L., W., and the rest; count up the novelists — S., T., D., R., G., H., and others of the tribe; consider the array of essayists, travellers, and naturalists, men and women of mark; and then ask whether Hunt, Parry, & Co. are surpassed by any of their contemporaries in their numerous issues, taking quantity, quality, and variety into the account. In offering this broadside programme of their performances, as bookmakers and booksellers, to the crowds of Jubilee week, they put forth a statement of indisputable facts; give a transcript of the record of the volumes they have issued, and their relations to eminent writers.

" Their achievements imply something more than an immediate and exclusive eye to the main chance.

18

It is evident that the honorable pursuit of profit is not with them the sole consideration. [O that it were !] They desire to connect their names with good literature, advanced thought, and the intellectual progress of the age. They would be known for their taste and liberal policy as well as for their mercantile success ; acting upon the principle that character as well as money is worth earning in the pursuits of trade and commerce. Without entering into comparisons, thus much is fairly to be inferred from their extended advertisement. It tells of results which imply the existence of the qualities we have attributed to them ; for without such qualities such results could not have been attained. The evidence of culture, judgment, sagacity, energy, boldness, tact, skill, and whatever else goes to the building up of a publishing house known at home and abroad for its magnitude and the extent and variety of its ventures, is literally such that he who runs may read and see that it is beyond controversy. This is not extravagant praise or mere compliment; but simply the statement of the truth as made manifest by the facts.

"In this general reference to Messrs. Hunt, Parry, & Co., we must not, in passing, omit an allusion to their periodicals. To them the public are indebted for the maintenance of the oldest Greek Quarterly, the agreeable and fresh weekly selections of ' Every

Tuesday,' the wide circulation and high character
for ability, diversity, and independence of the
'Adriatic Monthly,' and that leading magazine of
its class, ' The Buddhist.'

" In thus calling attention to a publishing house
whose imprint is known wherever the Greek language is spoken or read, we are pointing to what is
one of the leading concerns in a most important
branch of the business of the city, of which others
besides its proprietors may well be proud. Not
only has it grown with the growing culture of the
country, but it has encouraged home authors, and
spread far and wide the best productions of the best
writers on the other side of the Atlantic; thus giving it a claim to honorable consideration as holding
a high place among the beneficent agencies of the
advancing civilization of the world."

And a third chimes in : —

" The firm of Hunt, Parry, & Co., now almost
as familiar to the public under the new name as
under the old colors with which it sailed so long,
has been a bulwark and a rallying point for our
literature, on which book buyers as well as book
writers depended for many years. It has always
been active, but never so active as now. In another part of this paper, this house advertise their

principal publications for the past eighteen months. With little more amplification than a catalogue, the list fills a very considerable space; but it is when we come to appreciate quality as well as quantity that its full importance is realized. No other Athenian house could bulletin such a list of authors, beginning with L., and ranging along the varied types of our literature, from W., S., H., H., and L., to P., H., and A. Nor can any house exhibit such a list of English writers, with the added merit of the authors' sanction, as T., B., H., E., D., and R.

" Periodicals have come to be recognized as necessary tenders to the business of every book firm; but the monthlies and the quarterly, etc., etc., etc.

" Whatever may be the differing opinions after the experiences of this week, upon the commercial position and prospects of Athens and the success of her musical experiments, there can be no dispute as to our preëminence among Greek cities as a literary centre. Even Corinthians, bitterly as they may sneer at our Jubilee, are forced to read the works of Athenian authors and to supply their libraries with Athenian books. It would be impossible to estimate approximately the influence in producing the literary character of the city, its clustering of authors, its tone of society, of one great publishing house; but unquestionably that influence is very great."

An ill-timed modesty on the part of the firm of Hunt, Parry, & Co. has apparently prevented the publication of the fact, but it is well known in Athenian social circles that the eclipse which made the last summer famous, and which elicited so much interest throughout the scientific world, was not owing to the interposition of the moon between our planet and the sun, but was chiefly due to the temporary disappearance from this continent of the senior partner of the house of Hunt, Parry, & Co.

I do not say that the extracts which I have quoted, and others which I might quote, emanated from the same pen, or that that pen was held in the interest of Hunt, Parry, & Co., but I do say that on any other theory the correspondence of thought, of illustration, and even of language is not a little remarkable.

And if this theory be correct, if the house which has perhaps the reputation of being the most liberal, the most generous, and the most refined publishing house in this country, has attained that reputation by assiduously blowing its own trumpet while assiduously strangling its own authors, of what value is reputation?

A novel and striking illustration of my theme has just come to hand in the publication of Miss Mitbridge's "Letters." In 1754 she writes of Mr. Hunt: "He is a partner in the greatest publishing

house of Greece, and the especial patron of ———,
whom he found starving, and has made affluent by
his encouragement and liberality, for the great ro-
mancer is so nervous that he wants as much kindness
of management, as much mental nursing as a sick
child. I have never known a more charming person than Mr. Hunt."

The author to whom Miss Mitbridge refers is the
author of whose real or supposed wrongs I have
before spoken. If these publishers were indeed so
liberal towards him, the unanimity with which that
author's family and friends agree in attributing to
them the contrary policy is a singular proof of in-
gratitude to benefactors ; and Mr. Hunt may well
exclaim with the Prophet of old, " I have nour-
ished and brought up children, and they have rebelled against me."

I do not know what force these adulatory remarks may have upon the minds of others, but my
experience and my information are such that whenever I see in the newspapers a fresh ascription of
praise to the liberality of this house, I immediately
infer that the screw has been given another turn
on some unlucky author. The firm appears to me
in the similtude of evil-minded hens cackling their
noisy cut-cut-cut-ca-dah-cut over each new-laid egg,
designing to conceal from an uninquiring public
that, like those laymen denounced by Isaiah, they

" hatch cockatrices' eggs ; he that eateth of their eggs dieth, and that which is crushed breaketh out into a viper."

At a later period these general paragraphs began to converge around a particular point, and snugly nestled in among the literary items of religious newspapers may be found such announcements as this : —

" The public is threatened with a new book by the once redoubtable M. N., in which she is to narrate her tribulations, real or imaginary, with the eminent publishers, Hunt, Parry, & Co. Authors are very apt to have extravagant ideas of the popu - larity and profits of their books, unmindful of the fact that, generally, they are indebted to their pub- lishers for a large proportion of their fame, and it will take several books to convince the public that H., P., & Co. deal unfairly with their authors. Thus far, H., P., & Co. have kept quiet during M. N.'s attacks, but we hope the time will come when they will vindicate themselves."

And almost simultaneously, in another quarter of the heavens, appears a similar turtle-dove, its pin- feathers developed into well-defined plumage, but unquestionably a bird of the same brood : —

" M. N., once more famous than now, had a little ' unpleasantness' with her publishers, Hunt, Parry, & Co. In plain words, she accused them of cheating her out of some thousands of dollars by making false returns of sales of her books. Like many authors, she had become inordinately vain, and had extravagant ideas of the popularity of her books, and was, as is too often the case, unmindful of the fact that a large portion of what fame she then had (but has now lost) was made for her by these self-same publishers. She had a quarrel with them of eighteen months standing, but they would not even appear in self-defense ; what man would want to have an open quarrel with a woman ? To any one acquainted with the details of book publishing, the charge she brings against H., P., & Co. is simply absurd ; and besides, no business man would ever dare to suspect this publishing house to attempt such a system of petty cheating, and which, if attempted, would involve an amount of detail inconsistent with the end to be reached. H., P., & Co. are above the taint of suspicion. The truth is, M. N.'s books did not sell so well as she expected, and her pride (and her pocket) had a fall. It is known to us that an enormous outlay in advertising failed to make a remunerative sale on her last book. It fell dead on the market. It is now very quietly rumored that she has written a little volume which she proposes to call 'Little Men,' in which she describes her tribulations with the house of H., P., & Co. . . . M. N., you had better not! the public will not believe you."

The public will at least believe that, though a once redoubtable author, like Giant Pope in the Pilgrim's Progress, by reason of age, and also of the many shrewd brushes that he met with in his younger days, be grown crazy and stiff in his joints, he can at least sit in his cave's mouth, grinning at publishers as they go by, and biting his nails, because he cannot come at them!

It is not probable that these later paragraphs were actually written by the rose, but by some one who lives near the rose, and who takes roseate views of the situation.

When one has been introduced behind the scenes, these little touches go for what they are worth, but outside, they unquestionably, if imperceptibly, affect public opinion, and like an army of moral polyps build high the walls of lofty Rome. (A new species of polyps, the naturalist will say, but it answers my purpose.)

But while recognizing, to its fullest extent, the great power and prestige of a flourishing publishing house, and the great risk a writer runs in opposing it, I cannot bring myself to accept its invincibility,

or its infallibility, or its indispensability. Of course
a good reputation is, or ought to be, the sign of a
good character; but a thing which is wrong is
wrong, whatever be the reputation of him who does
it. A charge of wrong is to be met by denial. It
is not to dazzled out of sight in a general brilliancy.
When the course of our true love ceased to run
smooth, I supposed my pebble was the only obstacle
which my publishers' rivulet had ever known, and
I was dismayed accordingly. But if all the rocks
I have since discovered could be cast into one heap,
we should have a bigger monument than Joshua
made to mark the passage of Jordan. But the
monumenteers suffer in silence or speak with a
bated breath that cannot be heard outside their own
circle, while the flourishing firm keeps up such a
continuous tooting with its rams' horns as would
have flung flat the walls of Jericho had they been
twice as stout as they were. Undoubtedly it is not
wise always to make an outcry over your follies or
misfortunes. Neither is it wise always to go through
the world with a chip on your shoulder, challeng-
ing people to fillip it off. Yet we all admit that
there are times when short, sharp, and decisive resistance to aggression is the wisest plan. So also is
there a time to speak as well as a time to refrain
from speaking. There may be dignity, there may
be generosity, there may be prudence, or pusillanim-

ity, or selfishness in silence. There may be all in speech. Of this I am certain, if any of those writers who have escaped harm by their own skill, or any of those who have thought to escape further harm by silence had but given warning of the existence of rocks, some of us, with less skill, would have avoided that vicinage and might have had smooth sailing through the whole voyage. By their silence they have not only indirectly contributed to our disaster, but they have actually strengthened against us the hands of our natural foes, the publishers. They make it possible for a newspaper to say, in reference to the present difficulty, " As the house (of H., P., & Co.) has been in thriving existence for more than a quarter of a century, and has never before quarreled with an author, — or more correctly speaking, never had an author quarrel with it, — there will be a general disposition," and so forth. They thus directly increase the resistance which any succeeding author must overcome. " Nothing," says " The Nation " newspaper of January 13, 1770, in harsher language than I care to use, but we must take language as we find it, — " Nothing so promotes swindle as the readiness of the victims to pocket their losses, go their way with a sickly smile, and let the rogues begin again." But of course this must be left for each person to decide for himself. It is only that if one feels

moved in the spirit to bear witness against wrong
in any of the relations of life, there is nothing in
the height, or depth, or breadth, or brilliancy of any
reputation to overawe him. Nothing is real but
the right. There is no life but in truth. When
faith is lost, when honor dies, the man is dead.
Dead? He never was born. There never was
any such person. He was a mirage, an apparition.
The stars dim twinkle through his form.

As to the harm that may accrue to an author
from adopting the course which he counts wise, it
seems to me entirely insignificant. Nobody expects to go through the world intact, but we all
expect to do that which presents itself to be done.
If a writer has life in himself he will not easily die.
If he has not life in himself the sooner he dies the
better. If there is no life outside one charmed
circle,

> " Then am I dead to all the globe,
> And all the globe is dead to me."

Nothing is indispensable but a mind at peace with
itself. It is pleasant to celebrate the glory of those
you love, but better trudge comfortably across country on foot and alone, with all your worldly goods
knotted up in a yellow bandana than ride unwil-
lingly behind anybody's triumphal car.

So then, while it is undoubtedly best as a general
thing for an author to live at peace with publishers,

and sinners, there is also no reason why he should not make war if it is borne in upon him to do so.

But the only royal road to justice is for authors, in the beginning, to be intelligent, prompt, exact and exacting on all business matters which come within their scope. This seems a little thing, but it would work a revolution in the literary world. Let writers deal with publishers, not like women and idiots, but as business men with business men. If an author chooses to relinquish all pecuniary rewards from his books and to make an outright gift of the profits to his publishers, he may leave the whole matter in their hands ; but if he condescends to take any part in the spoils, he thereby becomes a business partner, and the only question is whether he shall be a good business man or a poor one. By not being prompt and intelligent, by neglecting to secure or to examine his accounts, or to correct them when they are wrong, or to understand them when they are obscure, he does not approve himself an unmercenary person ; he simply shows himself to be shambling and shiftless, and puts a direct temptation in his publisher's path. Many a servant would be honest if her careless mistress would not leave money lying about. Had I but used the ordinary care and caution which a lawyer, or a merchant, or a marketman brings to his business, this trouble doubtless would never have happened, and

we should all have been the happier for it. The
simple consciousness on the part of a publisher,
that an author is observant of what is visible, will
have a tendency to make him exact and upright
concerning what is invisible. An author should so
order his affairs that a publisher must make an
effort to be dishonest. On the contrary, he so
neglects them that a publisher must make an effort to be honest. Confidence and trust are excellent things and never more excellent than
when they have a solid basis of paper and ink. Do
the best he can there will still be points enough for
the author to exercise his trust on, but to do business wholly on the trust system is utterly childish.
No confidence can be more complete than was mine,
and none apparently can be founded on a more
honorable reputation. The confidential, friendly
way of conducting affairs is pretty and sentimental,
grateful to one's indolence and vanity and over fas-
tidiousness, and confirmatory of one's conviction
that he is too dainty and delicate to touch a bargain
with the tips of his fingers. But in fact we all do
take money for our work when we can get it ; we
want just as much money and money just as much
as other people — rather more — and, in sober truth,
the friction, the sacrifice of delicacy in keeping your
money affairs straight from day to day, is not for a
moment to be compared to the delicacy which may

be sacrificed by leaving them at the mercy of others. You run well for a while, but a day of reckoning is almost sure to come. The thriftless, hap-hazard way of bargaining or not bargaining, common among literary people, is the fruitful parent of uneasiness, anxiety, disappointment, and bitterness, before which delicacy must be rudely and ruthlessly brushed.

It is the same with women as with men, for in literature as in the gospel, there is neither male nor female. When a woman does any work for which she receives money she becomes so far a man, and passes immediately and inevitably under the yoke of trade. She has no right to demand a favorable judgment of her work because she is a woman, nor has she the least right to require that chivalry shall come in to help fix or secure her compensation. Trade laws know no more of gallantry than trade winds — and it is well they do not. Individuals and societies wheedle and flatter and threaten and torture according to the fashion, or passion, or panic of the hour, but under it all, the great, pitiless, unseen, inexorable law of the world holds from age to age, never relaxing its grasp, never revoking its decree, deaf to the wail of weakness, dumb to the cry of despair, forever and forever teaching with unrelenting persistency, *by* unrelenting persistency, the good and wholesome lesson that will be taught no other way.   Under this law there is no sex, no chivalry, no deference, no mercy. There is nothing but supply and demand ; nothing but buy and sell.   To him who understands it, and guides himself by it, it is a chariot of state bearing him on to fame and fortune.   To him who does not comprehend it and flings himself against it, it is a car of Juggernaut, crushing him beneath its wheels, without passion, but without pity.